Murder in the Grotto

LOTTIE SPRIGG COUNTRY HOUSE MYSTERY BOOK 2

MARTHA BOND

Lottie Sprigg Country House Mystery Series

* * *

Murder in the Library
Murder in the Grotto
Murder in the Maze

Chapter One

'I HOPE IT STOPS SNOWING SOON,' said Lord Buckley-Phipps as he stood at the breakfast room window and sipped his tea. 'This weather might put people off from attending the Christmas Fayre this afternoon.'

'The forecast suggests it will ease by lunchtime, my lord,' said the butler, Mr Duxbury.

'That's something to hope for, then.'

'I feel sorry for the men setting up out there,' said Mrs Moore. 'You'll make sure they're invited in for a mug of something warm once they're finished, won't you, Ivan?'

'Yes, I should think Lucinda will see to that.' He returned to his seat and began leafing through the newspaper.

Lottie finished her scrambled egg and toast and passed a few morsels to her corgi, Rosie, beneath the table. She was looking forward to the Fayre. It was an event she'd always enjoyed when she'd worked as a maid at Fortescue Manor. The staff were given the afternoon off and encouraged to join in with the festivities. Each year there was ice skating on the frozen lake, tobogganing on the hill, and pretty stalls selling food, drink and gifts. Lottie liked the Christmas carols sung by the local choir who lit their lanterns as the light faded in the winter afternoon.

Lottie now worked as a companion for Lady Buckley-Phipps' sister, Mrs Moore. The pair had travelled during the summer as Mrs Moore had attempted to secure her fourth marriage. The plan had fallen through, however, and they'd spent the past few months at Fortescue Manor with the Buckley-Phipps family.

'Good morning!' Barty Buckley-Phipps, the family's eldest child, arrived in the breakfast room. 'Is everyone excited?'

'More worried than excited, Barty,' said his father. 'I don't think this snow is going to stop.' He pointed a buttered knife at the window where thick flakes floated past.

'Of course it will stop, Father.' Barty lifted the lids off the serving dishes on the sideboard as he decided what to have for breakfast.

'The forecast certainly suggests so,' said the butler.

'There you go, Father, listen to Duxbury. He always talks sense.'

Lady Buckley-Phipps stepped into the room. She wore an indigo blue wool dress with long sleeves and silver trim on the low waist and collar.

'Very smart, Lucinda,' said Mrs Moore.

'Thank you, Roberta. Something smart yet warm is needed for today. We're going to be outside all afternoon. You're all still eating your breakfast?'

'Yes,' said her husband. 'We can't all be married ladies and get served in bed.'

'I asked Nelly to bring up breakfast earlier than usual. There's a lot to get done this morning.'

'They're outside doing it already, Lucinda,' said Lord Buckley-Phipps, gesturing with his knife again. 'What do you need to do?'

'Oversee it.' She turned to the butler. 'How's Mrs Palmer getting on with the mince pies, Duxbury?'

'I shall go downstairs and find out, my lady. Both she and Miss Hudson began making the pastry at six.'

'Good, hopefully they're on track, then.' The butler left the room and Lady Buckley-Phipps stepped over to the window. 'Golly, even more snow has fallen now. I hope people don't stay away.'

'That's what I'm worried about too,' said her husband through a mouthful of toast.

'We need a good attendance to support the mayor's charity,' said Lady Buckley-Phipps. 'It's been a challenging year for them. For some reason, they haven't been able to raise as much as in previous years. I've discussed it with the mayoress, Ruth Campbell, who confirmed it's been a difficult year. It seems people are less willing to put their hands in their pockets at the moment.'

'I blame taxes,' said her husband.

'Well, whatever the reason is, we've noticed the difference at Oswestry hospital. As one of the trustees on the board, I've been quite concerned about the reduction in funds. We usually receive a decent amount from the mayor's charity. That's why I proposed this year that all the proceeds from the Christmas Fayre would be donated to the mayor's charity.'

'Where have the proceeds gone in previous years?' asked Mrs Moore.

'They've been split between various local causes. But this year the mayor's charity will be the main beneficiary. The Lowton Chorley Ladies' Society have also undertaken some admirable fund-raising efforts to help the charity.'

'The Ladies' Society,' muttered Lord Buckley-Phipps. 'Never have I encountered such a crowd of meddling—'

'That's quite enough, Ivan,' scolded his wife. 'The mayoress is in the running to be the new chair of the Ladies'

3

Society. And don't forget you're good friends with her husband, the mayor.'

'I've got all the time in the world for Walter Campbell, but much less for his wife.'

'They'll be joining us here later, Ivan, so you need to be polite.'

'Of course I'll be polite! What do you take me for, Lucinda?'

'I know what you're like. Sometimes that face of yours gives you away.'

'There's nothing wrong with my face!'

'Mother's right,' said Barty. 'I can always tell what you're thinking from your expression, Father.'

'Is that so? What am I thinking about at the moment, then?'

'You're annoyed because we're discussing your facial expressions.'

'Correct!' He buttered another piece of toast. 'What a nonsense!'

Mr Duxbury returned to the room. 'I can confirm that the housekeeper and the cook are making good progress with the mince pies, my lady.'

'How many have they made?'

'About fifty, my lady.'

'Is that all?'

'I believe so, my lady.' The butler turned to Mrs Moore. 'I have some post for you here, Mrs Moore, which has been forwarded from your London address.'

'Thank you, Duxbury.' She put down her knife and fork and took the small pile of post from him. 'It's very kind of my dear housekeeper to keep on top of these things. These look completely dull, though.' She sifted through the envelopes.

'I shall have to visit the kitchen myself and join in with the mince pie making,' said Lady Buckley-Phipps. 'We need at least three hundred.'

'Three hundred?' said her husband. 'I don't like the thought of three hundred mince pies being scoffed on the premises. Crumbs will get dropped everywhere and encourage the rats.'

'I do wish you'd stop worrying about vermin, Ivan.'

'I worry about it because we have a problem with vermin, Lucinda.'

'Golly, Lottie,' said Mrs Moore. 'This envelope looks quite special, doesn't it?' The paper was thick and expensive looking. Mrs Moore's name and address had been written in elegant handwriting on the front. 'There's certainly something distinctive about this one.'

Lottie watched her open the envelope with a knife, then pull out a piece of card. It looked like an invitation. Mrs Moore's eye scanned over it. Then they widened and her mouth dropped open. 'Well, I never!' She placed a hand on her chest. 'Would you believe it? I've never been so... I'm simply overwhelmed!'

'What is it, Roberta?' asked Lady Buckley-Phipps.

'I'm quite taken aback! And it's taking a moment to sink in.'

'What is?'

'This invitation I've received. I've been invited to a Christmas ball in London.'

'Very nice,' replied her sister. 'And who's hosting it?'

'Would you believe it, Lucinda, but our king and queen! I've been invited to a Christmas ball at Buckingham Palace!'

Lady Buckley-Phipps' eyebrows raised halfway up her forehead. Then she sank into a chair at the breakfast table. '*You*, Roberta? You've been invited to Buckingham Palace? Why?'

'I don't know. Isn't it funny? Fancy little old me being

invited to an event like that. I suppose I've got to know a number of people in London society now, and my name must have become known enough to receive a personal invitation from their majesties.'

'Just because you know some people?'

'Yes. Important people.'

'But you haven't even got a title!'

'There's no need to bring snobbery into this, Lucinda.'

'I'm not being snobby! I just thought you had to have a title or be married to someone important to get invited to such events.'

'Titles aren't everything, Lucinda. We're living in modern times now. I've clearly made my mark on London during the past few seasons there.'

'By doing what?' Lady Buckley-Phipps looked incredibly put out, and Mrs Moore seemed to be enjoying it.

'I work much harder than you realise, Lucinda.'

'So when is the ball?'

'The 23rd of December. It looks like you and I will be returning to London for Christmas, Lottie.'

Lottie had little wish to return to London. She'd been looking forward to spending Christmas at Fortescue Manor. But Mrs Moore was excited about the invitation so Lottie knew she had to go along with it. 'How exciting!' she said.

'The 23rd of December is eight days away,' said Lord Buckley-Phipps. 'Let's hope they clear the railway line between London and Shrewsbury by then. I've just read in the newspaper that it's been blocked by the latest snowfall. You're lucky the invitation reached you before that happened.'

'Oh goodness! I hope they clear it soon. I don't want to miss the Christmas ball at Buckingham Palace!'

Chapter Two

EVERYONE GATHERED in the drawing room after lunch. The staff had changed into their best clothes for the Fayre and joined the Buckley-Phipps family as they waited for the mayor and mayoress of Oswestry to arrive. The younger Buckley-Phipps children were accompanied by a team of nannies and governesses who were failing in their efforts to keep them calm and quiet.

The children were enthralled by the large Christmas tree at the end of the room. It was covered with twinkling lights and colourful ornaments. Lottie felt a skip of excitement as she saw the hundreds of presents piled around the tree. These were gifts for the village children. It was a Christmas Fayre tradition that the mayor dressed up as Father Christmas and handed out the presents. A red and green tent had been erected for this purpose and the new footman, Jack, was already dressed up as a Christmas elf to assist Father Christmas. Lottie couldn't help smiling at his outfit. He looked a little self-conscious in his red and green jacket, green tights, a red pointed hat and shoes with shiny bells on. He met Lottie's eye, and she glanced away, embarrassed he'd noticed her looking at him.

'You haven't changed your clothes, Mrs Palmer,' said the housekeeper, Miss Hudson. The housekeeper wore a sombre, high-necked dress which was remarkably similar to her work clothing. The cook wore a flour-covered apron over a striped dress with the sleeves rolled up. Her bonnet flopped into her eyes.

'I haven't found the chance yet, Miss Hudson,' she said. 'I've never baked so many mince pies in all my days!'

'You did very well to bake three hundred,' said Lady Buckley-Phipps.

'Thank you, my lady. Although I must say I don't want to see another mince pie until next Christmas.'

Lottie sipped the mulled wine, which was warm and richly flavoured with orange and spices.

'Isn't this wine lovely?' said Mrs Moore. 'It's really getting me into the festive spirit! And I can't wait to have one of those mince pies.'

The cook groaned at the mention of the words. She was a recent addition to the staff of Fortescue Manor and hadn't yet experienced the challenges of cooking for the household at Christmas time.

The doorbell rang and Mr Duxbury went to answer it. Lady Buckley-Phipps smoothed her dress and adjusted her husband's tie.

'There's no need to make such a fuss, dear,' said her husband. 'It's only Walter and his wife.'

'They're attending in their capacity as mayor and mayoress. We must respect that.'

Moments later, the butler showed the mayor and mayoress into the room. 'Mr and Mrs Walter Campbell, mayor and mayoress of Oswestry.'

Walter Campbell was a broad, jolly-faced man with heavy jowls and a thick, grey moustache. He wore a three-cornered hat, a red velvet robe and layers of white lace at his collar and cuffs. A heavy gold mayoral chain was draped across his shoulders and chest.

'Lord Buckley-Phipps!' The two men shook hands and gave each other a hearty slap on the shoulder. 'You've met my dear wife, Ruth, before, haven't you?'

'I have indeed.' Lord Buckley-Phipps took a bow. 'It's a pleasure to see you again, Mrs Campbell.'

'Thank you, my lord.' She was a tall lady with a haughty expression and wavy hair which looked artificially dark. She also wore a red mayoral robe, but her gold chain was smaller and more delicate than the one her husband wore.

'I suppose I should take my hat off,' said the mayor. 'The trouble is, I enjoy wearing it too much. I don't get the opportunity to wear my full mayoral garb very often.'

'Make the most of it, Walter,' said Lord Buckley-Phipps. 'Once you've officially opened the Fayre, you'll have to get your Father Christmas outfit on.'

'Ah yes, that little task.'

'One which your predecessors have always enjoyed. I'm told it's the highlight of every Oswestry mayor's tenure.'

'In which case, I can't wait to get on with it. Ho ho ho!'

Lady Buckley-Phipps presented the mayor and his wife with a glass of mulled wine each. 'This will help, I'm sure, Mr Campbell.'

'I'm sure it will! Let's raise a glass to the Fortescue Manor Christmas Fayre!'

Everyone raised their glasses, then took a drink.

Lottie noticed the cook, Mrs Palmer, didn't have a drink. Instead, her arms were folded across her ample bosom and she was glaring at the mayoress.

Chapter Three

ONCE THE MULLED wine was finished, everyone left the drawing room and went to the boot room to put on warm coats, scarves, gloves, hats and boots. Then they stepped out into the snow-covered grounds of Fortescue Manor. They were presented with a beautiful sight. The snow had stopped falling, and the sun had emerged from behind the clouds to bathe the winter landscape in golden light.

The frozen lake shimmered, and Lottie couldn't wait to skate on it. Encircling the lake were the food, drink and gift stalls. Their bright awnings were decorated with colourful bunting and festive ornaments.

Lottie and Rosie followed everyone along a path to the Fayre entrance which was marked with a section of red ribbon. An excited crowd was waiting for the event to open.

Mildred the maid joined Lottie. The pair had been friends since they had first begun working together at Fortescue Manor. 'This is my favourite time of year!' said Mildred. A striped woollen hat was pulled down over her red hair and she'd wrapped a long scarf around her neck and shoulders several times. 'All my family are going to be here. Mother's

10

even closed the laundry for the afternoon. Shall we go tobogganing together?'

'I'd love to!' said Lottie.

Mildred dashed off to find her family and Lottie and Rosie were joined by the three Jack Russell dogs who lived at the house. Rosie had been wary of them to begin with, but all four dogs got on well now. Lottie laughed as she watched them dash away from the path and roll together in the fresh snow.

'It must be so much fun being a dog, don't you think, Lottie?' said Barty. 'All that freedom to run around being silly with no one judging you.'

'Yes, it must be nice. You have to hope you have a nice owner to look after you, though.'

'Now that's a good point. And I suppose I've done my fair share of running around and being silly.'

Barty had been well known for getting into scrapes. Earlier in the year, he'd been kicked out of Oxford University for keeping the college dean's daughter out all night. Since then, however, he'd managed to talk his way into being readmitted. He'd returned to university in September and his parents had recently received a letter commending their son for his hard work during the term. Lottie had known Barty since he was fifteen and she had seen him change from a feckless youth into an almost-sensible young gentleman.

'Let's hope the mayor hurries up and gets the ribbon cut,' said Barty as they reached the Fayre entrance. 'We're all impatient to be getting on with it!'

Lord and Lady Buckley-Phipps and the mayor and mayoress had now been joined by a man in a smart overcoat and fur hat.

'Who's he?' Lottie asked Barty.

'Frederick Campbell,' said Barty. 'You've not heard of him?'

'Yes, his name rings a bell now. He's a businessman, isn't he?'

'Yes. He runs a limousine hire company, and he owns some restaurants and a small department store in Oswestry. He's also the mayor's brother.'

'Is he? I suppose the surname is a clue. And now you've told me, I can see the family resemblance.'

'He's done a lot of work for the Fayre,' said Barty. 'He's supplied the ice skates and sledges and also provided a number of the stalls. He hasn't charged Mother and Father a penny for it. He told them he was keen to do what he could to help the mayor's charity.'

'Ladies and gentlemen!' The loud volume of the mayor's voice from the megaphone made Lottie startle. 'It gives me great pleasure to declare the Fortescue Manor Christmas Fayre open! What's that?' The mayoress was talking to him. 'The ribbon? Oh, I need to cut the ribbon. Where are the scissors?'

'I don't think it's occurred to him to put the megaphone down while they're sorting this out,' said Barty.

Eventually, the scissors were handed to him.

'I have the scissors now!' declared the mayor to the crowd. 'And I shall now cut the ribbon... there, it's done!' This was met with a round of applause. 'Now go and enjoy yourselves! And a very merry Christmas to you all!'

'LET'S GO ICE SKATING, LOTTIE!' said Mrs Moore. 'I used to ice skate a lot as a girl, but it's been almost a year since I last found the chance. Shall we give it a go?'

'Yes! Although I'm not very good.'

'You'll soon get the hang of it.'

'Mrs Moore?' Frederick Campbell, in his smart overcoat and fur hat, joined them. He was a broad-shouldered man with a jowled face which had probably once been handsome.

'Mr Campbell! You remembered my name?'

'How could I forget it?'

'Oh!' Mrs Moore blushed a little and introduced Lottie.

'It's a pleasure to meet you and your dog, Miss Sprigg. A Pembroke Welsh Corgi?' He patted Rosie on the head. 'One of my favourite breeds.' He turned back to Mrs Moore. 'The Christmas Fayre at Fortescue Manor is the highlight of every festive season, wouldn't you say? And all for a worthy cause. The mayor's charity has struggled this year. I've made some extra-large donations to support it.'

'How lovely of you, Mr Campbell.'

'And I don't believe I've seen you since last year's

Christmas Fayre, Mrs Moore. Do you only ever grace us with your presence at Christmas time?'

'Oh no, I've been here since the summer.'

'The summer? And our paths haven't crossed?'

'They haven't.'

'You didn't even call in at one of my restaurants?'

'It's been terribly remiss of me, Mr Campbell.'

'Well, you must call in and mention my name.'

'I shall try to find the time to do so before I return to London.'

'You're going to be in London for Christmas?'

'I've received an invitation to a Christmas ball at Buckingham Palace.'

'Buckingham Palace! Are you able to take a guest with you?'

'If you're volunteering yourself, Mr Campbell, I'm sure your wife wouldn't approve.'

'Oh, she needn't know about it.' He chuckled. 'I've always wanted to go to Buckingham Palace. I'm sure you'll have a wonderful time.'

'I will. Although I shall miss spending Christmas here at Fortescue Manor.'

'I'm sure you will.' He glanced around them. 'This has always been a special place for me.'

'Am I right in recalling you had family who once worked here, Mr Campbell?'

'You recall correctly! My great-grandfather was a valet to the then-Lord Buckley-Phipps.'

'That must have been some time ago.'

'Why? How old do you think I am, Mrs Moore?'

'Oh! I didn't mean it like that, I—'

He chuckled again. 'I'm only joking with you. You're right, I think it was about seventy years ago now. And thankfully, subsequent generations of my family haven't had to work in service.'

'You're a social climber, Mr Campbell.'

He laughed. 'You're a fine one to talk with your invitation to Buckingham Palace! Anyway, I could stand here and chat with you all day, Mrs Moore, but I really must be getting on. I want to pop up to the house and laugh at my brother in his Father Christmas outfit.'

'I can imagine that's a sight for sore eyes! It was lovely to see you again, Mr Campbell, and thank you for all your wonderful work on the Fayre this year.'

'Oh, it's a pleasure. I enjoy it. And it keeps me out of trouble.'

'I can't imagine you getting in trouble, Mr Campbell!' They both laughed, then he went on his way.

'What a charming man,' said Mrs Moore to Lottie. 'Isn't it a shame he's married? Anyway, let's get on with some ice skating.'

Chapter Five

THEY WALKED to the frozen lake and Mrs Moore surveyed the skaters through her lorgnette. Several skaters were unsteady on their feet and clung to each other for support. Others took regular tumbles, laughing as they went. A few people were quite accomplished, and Lottie admired how they weaved effortlessly around everyone else.

Lottie instructed Rosie to wait at the side of the lake, then she and Mrs Moore strapped skates onto their boots with leather straps and buckles.

Lottie cautiously followed Mrs Moore onto the ice. She stood for a moment with her arms outstretched and her knees bent, trying to get used to the slippery surface. Then, slowly and carefully, she began to nudge one foot forward and then the other. Mrs Moore was doing better, despite wearing a heavy blue coat which almost reached her ankles. She was moving faster than Lottie but didn't look particularly stable.

'Would it help if you held my hand?' asked Mrs Moore. 'Perhaps we can help each other with our balance.'

They gripped hands, and both skated forward. 'I think

you can probably go a little faster than that, Lottie,' said Mrs Moore.

'I'm not sure I can!'

Edward the footman greeted them as he skated past. He seemed happy he could enjoy the Fayre while his fellow footman, Jack, was having to dress as an elf and assist Father Christmas.

Once they'd completed a lap of the lake, Lottie felt her confidence growing. She passed Rosie, who fortunately remained contentedly at the edge of the lake.

Lottie tried pushing each foot further and longer. Before long, she felt the pleasurable sensation of gliding. She let go of Mrs Moore's hand and felt proud that she was skating properly. The breeze was cold on her face and she enjoyed the sound of her skates scraping along the ice. Her speed increased, then Lottie began to panic. How could she stop once she'd got going? The worry made her body tense, and her feet slid out from beneath her. She could do nothing to stop the fall, but her thick coat cushioned the knock.

'Lottie!' said Mrs Moore. 'Are you alright?'

'Yes, I'm fine!' Like everyone else who fell, she was laughing. It was probably from embarrassment and relief at not being hurt.

Mrs Moore helped her back up. 'Just keep going, Lottie. You're doing well!'

Mrs Moore skated on. Despite the fall, Lottie felt pleased with the progress she was making. As she reached the place where Rosie sat, she saw Mildred had joined her dog. She gave them both a wave, almost losing her balance as she did so.

'Mind how you go!' said Mildred with a laugh.

Lottie had lost sight of Mrs Moore now, she was lost among the crowd of skaters. A lady zoomed past and Lottie recognised her as the mayoress, Ruth Campbell. Her mayoral robes flowed behind her, leaving a breeze in her wake. She wove in and out of the skaters ahead, then perfected an elegant circle before continuing on her way. It was an impressive display, but Lottie thought the mayoress was showing off a little.

Another lady passed by, skating sedately. 'Good afternoon, Lottie,' she said as she passed. It was the housekeeper, Miss Hudson. Then Barty passed by. He was doing a good speed, but his arms and legs floundered as he struggled to control them. Lottie couldn't help smiling, certain he was going to take a tumble before long.

Moments later, she heard a cry and turned to see a lady in a blue coat lying on the other side of the lake. A streak of red flashed away. Had the mayoress knocked someone over?

Lottie realised it was Mrs Moore. She skated over to her as quickly as she could, wobbling and steadying herself along the way. By the time she reached her employer, a man and two women were helping her to her feet.

'Mrs Moore! Are you alright?'

'Yes, I'm fine, thank you, Lottie. Just a little bruised.' She glanced over at the far side of the lake where the mayoress was perfecting another swift turn. 'She came too close and distracted me.'

'Mrs Campbell knocked into you?' Lottie asked.

'It was an accident. Just a tiny brush of her elbow, but it was enough to knock me over like a ninepin.'

'The cheek of it!'

'I don't think she realised.'

'Auntie!' Barty joined them. 'Are you alright?'

'Fine thank you, Barty.'

'Are you hurt?'

'Slightly bruised. But I'll be alright.'

'That mayoress is a menace,' said Barty. 'She just expects everyone to get out of her way.'

'I saw what happened!' said a stout grey-haired lady. 'We're

18

trying to find Frederick Campbell to ask if he can have a word with her. Not only is he in charge of the ice skating, but he's also her brother-in-law. Hopefully she'll listen to him.'

'I really don't want too much fuss made,' said Mrs Moore.

'She didn't even check to see if you were alright!'

'No. Perhaps she didn't notice or perhaps she's just...'

'Rude!'

'Yes, it could be that. I'm happy to forget about it though. Instead, I think a nice mug of hot chocolate is in order.'

Chapter Six

MILDRED DASHED over with Rosie as Lottie, Mrs Moore and Barty were taking off their ice skates.

'What a nasty fall!' she said. 'Are you alright, Mrs Moore?'

'Absolutely fine. Thank you, Mildred. I know you and Lottie are keen to go tobogganing. Why don't you go off together and do that now?'

'Will you be alright, Mrs Moore?' Lottie asked.

'I'll keep an eye on Auntie,' said Barty.

'I really don't need anyone keeping an eye on me!'

'I need to make sure you drink plenty of hot chocolate.'

'Alright then.' Mrs Moore laughed. 'I think I can live with that. Have fun tobogganing, girls!'

'We will!'

Lottie, Mildred and Rosie made their way through the snow to the hill beyond the lake. Whoops of delight carried on the breeze as people whizzed down the slope on sledges.

'Mrs Moore took quite a tumble,' said Mildred as they climbed the hill. 'The mayoress knocked into her and didn't even stop or apologise or anything! The mayoress is very rude. She thinks she's better than everyone now her husband is the mayor. But really, she's just Mrs Campbell. My mother describes her as a local busybody.'

'Why?'

'Apparently she does lots of work for local causes, but not because she genuinely cares about them. She does it because she thinks it makes her look good. That's what my mother says, anyway.'

'I think it's nice that she does things for charity.'

'Yes, it is nice. But she could do it without having to tell everybody about it, couldn't she? I suppose I don't know Mrs Campbell, but I do trust my mother's word.'

'I think I probably trust her word as well, Mildred,' said Lottie with a smile.

They were panting by the time they reached the top of the hill. A boy stood there with the sledges.

'Mind how you go,' he said. 'The temperature's dropping now and the snow's getting icy from where everyone's been sledging down it.'

'We'll be careful, won't we, Lottie?' said Mildred, taking a sledge from him. It was a long sledge which could seat three people. 'Do you want to drive, or shall I drive, Lottie?'

'You can't drive a sledge,' said the boy.

'What else do I describe it as?'

'I don't know.' He shrugged. 'Steer it? You can't steer these ones very well, though.'

Lottie glanced down the hill. It was steeper than she remembered.

'Let's go,' said Mildred, climbing onto the front of the sledge. She sat down and picked up the rope at the front. Lottie felt sure the rope would offer little help with steering, but she chose not to say anything. She sat behind Mildred, then lifted Rosie and placed her between the two of them.

Lottie wrapped an arm around Rosie and clung to the sledge with her other hand, hoping this would be enough to stay on. The slope looked even steeper from this angle and the boy's warning about the ice rang in her ears.

'I'll give you a push to get you started,' said the boy.

'Ready?' asked Mildred. Lottie could hear the excitement in her voice.

Lottie didn't have time to reply before the boy sent them off with an almighty shove.

Rosie barked with excitement as the toboggan picked up speed. Mildred was laughing, and Lottie felt the rush of wind in her ears. For a brief moment, she was able to appreciate Fortescue Manor nestled in the snowy valley and all the people in the grounds enjoying themselves. But then the sledge raced on faster, and her thoughts turned to staying on.

The runners whooshed on the snow, and they encountered little bumps here and there which threatened to unseat them. Mildred whooped with delight. But it wasn't long before she went quieter.

'Oh, Lottie! We're going too fast!'

'We are.'

Lottie clung onto Rosie and the wooden seat as best she could.

'There's nothing I can do to stop this!' said Mildred.

The sledge went faster, and the ride grew bumpier.

'How do I stop?' cried out Mildred.

'We'll stop at the bottom.'

'But we're going to hit the stalls!'

'We won't.'

But to Lottie's alarm, it looked as though they might. The slope was levelling out now but their speed hadn't slowed.

Rosie's tongue rolled out of her mouth happily. She was

clearly enjoying the ride. Lottie was more focused on the group of people standing by a stall ahead of them.

Mildred took matters into her own hands. 'Mind out of the way!' she called out.

The hill had almost ended, but the sledge continued.

Lottie grimaced as she watched the people ahead of them scatter. More worryingly, the sledge was now heading directly for the side of the stall. They were going to hit the trestle table and the awning. The entire stall was going to collapse onto them, and someone was surely going to be hurt.

'Oh no!' cried out Mildred.

The sledge jolted. They'd hit a mound of snow at the foot of the slope. The toboggan pitched to one side, and Lottie, Mildred, and Rosie tumbled off into the snow.

Rosie was the first to her feet, barking excitedly. Lottie lay there recovering her breath and relieved they'd avoided hitting the stall.

Mildred laughed. 'That was enormous fun! Shall we go again?'

'Later. Maybe,' said Lottie. 'I need some time to recover from that. But you're right, it was fun.' As she got to her feet, she realised she'd enjoyed it after all.

The new maid, Nelly, ran over to them.

'How did you manage to go so fast?' she said. 'I thought you were going to hit the gingerbread stall!'

'So did we!' said Mildred.

'Have you been to the grotto yet?'

'No, not yet.'

'You must go! It looks beautiful. It's been filled with candles and paper lanterns. We've just looked around it.'

'But isn't it spooky?' said Mildred.

'Yes, everyone says the grotto is spooky, but it doesn't look spooky today because of the way it's been lit.'

'Alright, then. What do you think, Lottie?'

Lottie was familiar with the grotto and agreed that it was a bit spooky. But she also wanted to see it lit up with festive lights.

'Yes, let's go,' she said. 'The walk will give us a chance to recover our nerves.'

Chapter Seven

To reach the grotto, Lottie, Rosie and Mildred had to walk past the lake and take a path which led down to where the grotto lay at the foot of the slope. The little grotto was set in the hillside and had been constructed about two hundred years ago.

'I haven't been to the grotto for a long time,' said Mildred.

'I visited it in the summer,' said Lottie, 'but not since then. It's a very pretty place that someone has spent a lot of time on. But I always get a shiver down my spine when I visit.'

'Me too!' said Mildred. 'And the story of the grotto hermit doesn't help either.'

'I remember a story about the hermit,' said Lottie. 'But I can't remember the details.'

'According to my grandmother, he was a miserable man who lived in the village. One day, some children accidentally hit him with a ball they were playing with and he cursed them and their families. The following day, they were all dead!'

'Oh dear. Really?'

'After that, the villagers hounded him out with flaming torches and dogs. And then, for some reason, Lord Buckley-

Phipps took pity on him. Not the Lord Buckley-Phipps we've got now, but one who lived over one hundred years ago. He didn't believe the miserable man had cursed anyone. He said they'd died from cholera instead. So he said the man could live in the grotto. What a place to live! It's just a cave, isn't it? I suppose he must have cooked his food on the fire, but where did he get his food from? Maybe he poached it from the estate. Or maybe Lord Buckley-Phipps gave him something, I don't know. Anyway, apparently he lived as a hermit in the grotto for fifty years.'

'For that long?'

'That's what my grandmother said. And hardly anybody saw him. But he was said to walk around the grounds at night, and if someone did ever set eyes on him, then they would be cursed with bad luck.'

'Such as what?'

'Any animals they owned would die.'

'Oh no, that's awful! Surely it can't be true?'

'I don't know. It's the story my grandmother told us.'

'Do you know what happened to him in the end?'

'He died of old age in the grotto.'

Lottie shuddered. 'He died in there? I didn't realise that.'

'And it's said that when they examined his body afterwards, they found he had no heart.'

Lottie couldn't help bursting into laughter. 'No heart? How could he possibly have survived with no heart?'

'I don't know,' Mildred shrugged. 'The story made sense to me as a girl, but I can understand people questioning it these days. It sounds like a bit of nonsense now, doesn't it? Maybe there was a man who lived in the grotto for a little bit. But he probably did have a heart, didn't he? It's impossible not to have one. And he probably wasn't there for fifty years. Perhaps the Buckley-Phipps family knows more about the story? It's not my place to ask them, though.'

'I'll ask Barty about it,' said Lottie. 'I'm sure he's heard the story before. It would have been one of his ancestors who allowed the man to live in the grotto.'

'Whatever the exact story is,' said Mildred, 'everyone now says the grotto has been cursed by the hermit with no heart.'

'So what else has happened in the grotto?'

'My grandmother said a shepherd was found in there after sheltering from bad weather. He looked dead when they found him, but he wasn't. Instead, he just lay in a stupor for the rest of his days. He couldn't speak or do anything. Almost the same as being dead, really. My grandmother said he'd seen so much evil that he never recovered.'

'Is that really true?'

Mildred shrugged. 'Who knows? It's a good story though, isn't it? And there's definitely something spooky about the grotto.'

Lottie nodded. 'There is.'

'This is the first time I've known it to be decorated for Christmas. Apparently it was Frederick Campbell's suggestion. He's done a lot of the organising this year, hasn't he? And I'm looking forward to seeing if it's as good as Nelly described.'

They reached the arched cave-like entrance of the grotto. They were met with an enchanting display of flickering candles and colourful paper lanterns.

'It looks beautiful!' said Mildred. They stepped inside and admired the patterns on the walls made of thousands of little shells. 'Don't they look pretty all lit up like this?'

The last time Lottie had visited the grotto, Rosie had remained by the entrance. But today, she joined them inside. The festive lighting seemed to make the place more appealing to her.

'There's a little passageway at the back, isn't there?' said

Mildred, walking past the flickering candles to a dark recess on the right.

Lottie followed, but did so cautiously. It felt strange that only she, Mildred, and Rosie were here. Perhaps other people were avoiding the grotto because of the old stories.

'It looks lovely!' said Mildred. Lottie joined her and could see down the dark passageway. A few candles had been placed here, too.

'Does it lead to somewhere?' asked Lottie.

'No,' said Mildred. 'I've always wondered that, but apparently it doesn't lead anywhere. It's just a little passageway to give you the creeps. Maybe it was the hermit's bedroom?' She laughed.

Lottie ran a hand over the bumpy, intricately patterned wall. 'It must have been some job working on this,' she said. 'With no light as well. They must have worked by candlelight back then.'

'I wonder how many people it took to decorate it?'

The air inside the grotto was always cold and damp. Lottie imagined it was what a grave might feel like. And when that thought entered her mind, all thoughts of Christmas cheer seemed to evaporate.

'Let's go and do something else,' she said, keen to get out into the fresh afternoon air again.

'Don't you want to look around some more?'

'No, I think I've had enough. I'd like to go and have some hot chocolate to warm up.'

'Alright then,' said Mildred.

Lottie felt relieved as they left the grotto and stepped out into the snow again.

As they walked back up the path towards the Fayre, they saw two figures approaching. One wore a bright red cloak.

'Look who it is,' muttered Mildred. 'The show-off mayoress.'

She was walking with a smartly dressed, fair-haired gentleman who Lottie hadn't seen before. The pair were in deep conversation. Lottie smiled at them, but Mrs Campbell merely gave her and Mildred a brief glance.

'Do you know who the mayoress was with?' Lottie asked Mildred once they'd passed the pair.

'No. Never seen him before.'

'Whoever he was, their conversation seemed a bit serious, didn't it?'

Chapter Eight

At the mince pie stall, Lottie found Mrs Moore chatting to an auburn-haired lady in a fur-trimmed coat. The carol singers were performing *O Come, All Ye Faithful* and Mildred went off to watch them.

'Hello Lottie,' said Mrs Moore. 'How was the tobogganing?'

'Lots of fun. Then Mildred and I went to see the grotto. It's been lit with candles and Christmas lanterns and it looks beautiful.'

'That sounds pretty, I shall have to go and see it. This is Mrs Lily Granger and she's been telling me all about the Lowton Chorley Ladies' Society.' Mrs Moore followed this with a polite smile which suggested she'd already heard too much about it. 'This is my assistant, Miss Lottie Sprigg,' she said to the lady.

'It's lovely to meet you, Miss Sprigg.' Mrs Granger looked about forty-five and had pencilled eyebrows, red lips and a receding chin. 'I've just been telling Mrs Moore how the Ladies' Society has been helping Frederick Campbell with organising the Christmas Fayre. It's such an important event to raise funds for good causes. I'm proud to add that my son, Philip, works at Russell Bank and has persuaded the company to make a generous donation too.'

'How lovely,' said Mrs Moore. She turned to Lottie. 'Mrs Granger has been telling me all about the power struggle in the Ladies' Society.'

'Power struggle?' Mrs Granger laughed. 'Oh no, nothing of the sort! We're just trying to organise ourselves at the moment. It's all perfectly good-natured.'

'The current chair of the Ladies' Society has become incapacitated due to old age,' Mrs Moore explained to Lottie. 'A vote for her successor has just been held and the result was split equally between the two candidates.'

'That's right,' said Mrs Granger. 'I'm one of them.'

'And the other one is Mrs Campbell,' said Mrs Moore.

'Is that so?' said Lottie. She struggled to find this particularly interesting.

'I don't think Mrs Campbell expected me to get as many votes as her,' said Mrs Granger. 'I think she assumed she'd win the vote because she's a mayoress now. She's only a mayoress in name, I should add. And that's because her husband is the mayor. Her role doesn't actually have any official duties.'

'How will it be decided who becomes the chair?' asked Lottie.

'We're going to hold another vote. And, with a bit of luck, I'll win this time.'

'From what I've seen of Mrs Campbell, I can't imagine her being happy about that,' said Mrs Moore.

'No, but she can console herself with the fact she's the mayoress. She and her husband have had a good year. They moved into a new house, it's actually the former vicarage. Do you know it?'

'Yes, by the church?' said Mrs Moore. 'It's a lovely place. Quite large. Do they have a big family?'

'No. They have no family. Only themselves to worry about.' She gave a thin smile. 'And you must have seen Mrs Campbell speeding about the village in her new motor car.'

'I can't say that I have,' said Mrs Moore.

'Well you will now that I've mentioned it. Anyway, that's enough about them. Now, what do you say about joining us, Mrs Moore?'

'The Lowton Chorley Ladies' Society?'

'Absolutely.'

'I would love to, but I travel quite a bit and my main home is in London.'

'Even better!'

'Really?'

'Yes. I'm sure you could do valuable work for us in London, Mrs Moore.'

Lottie noticed her employer's face fall. 'Really?'

'Oh yes. There are a lot of influential people in London, and they all need to know about our good works. The more we can persuade important people to support our work raising money for charities, the better.'

'I see. Well, I do travel quite a bit as well.'

'Even better, Mrs Moore! You must meet many prominent people on your travels too. You could be an extremely good ambassador for the Lowton Chorley Ladies' Society.'

'I shall bear it in mind, Mrs Granger.'

'Wonderful. I shall call on you in a few days to discuss it further.'

'I can't wait.'

'Now, I'm going to visit the grotto. I've heard it's been beautifully decorated this year.'

'Oh dear, Lottie,' said Mrs Moore once Mrs Granger had left. 'I can't say I have much interest in getting involved with the Ladies' Society.'

'Why not if they do so much good work?'

'I like the idea of doing good work, Lottie, and I like to donate to charities on a regular basis. But I don't want to be in a group. They always end up falling out with each other. Mrs Granger was trying to play down the competition for votes to become the next chair, but I think you and I both know, Lottie, that the rivalry in these things can get quite vindictive. It can become a distraction from the good work, can't it? It's too adversarial for my liking. Would you like a mince pie? We've been stood by the stall for a while and not sampled them yet.'

'Thank you, I'd love one.'

The mince pie had a perfect buttery crust and a richly fruited interior. Lottie dropped a little piece for Rosie to sample.

'Mrs Palmer has done an excellent job with these,' said Mrs Moore. 'I think we need two more. What do you say?'

Chapter Nine

'I HOPE you haven't eaten all the mince pies, Auntie,' said Barty as he joined Lottie, Rosie and Mrs Moore.

'This is only my second, Barty. You cheeky young man.'

'Isn't this a wonderful Christmas Fayre? I've just enjoyed a nice glass of mulled wine. And you'll never guess who I bumped into at the drinks stall.'

'Who?' asked Lottie

'None other than Evelyn Abercromby. Can you believe it?'

Evelyn Abercromby was the daughter of Lord and Lady Abercromby who lived on the neighbouring Clarendon Park estate. The Buckley-Phipps family and the Abercrombys had been locked in a bitter feud for nearly three hundred years. The feud had worsened recently after the murder of their son Percy at Fortescue Manor.

'Evelyn Abercromby is here?' said Mrs Moore. 'That's a surprise.'

'I almost didn't recognise her,' said Barty. 'I would have walked straight past her if she hadn't stopped me and said hello. She was wearing a big hat, a thick coat, and a scarf wrapped around the lower part of her face. You would never have guessed it was her! She wasn't here for long, but it was nice to see her again. Her parents don't know she was here. I think they'd be a bit upset about it.'

'I imagine they would be,' said Mrs Moore.

Lottie recalled Barty's fondness for Evelyn Abercromby when she'd visited Fortescue Manor with her family in the summer.

'Evelyn told me she'd always wanted to come to the Christmas Fayre here, and this is the first time she's been. And, fortunately, she doesn't bear me any ill will.'

'That's quite surprising when you consider what happened to her brother,' said Lottie.

'Yes, it is. I suppose she's sensible enough to realise that it wasn't my fault. So she's keeping well. And seeing her has been the highlight of the Christmas Fayre.'

'So have you arranged to see her again?' asked Mrs Moore.

'No. I'd like to, but I'm wary of suggesting it. She has every right to want nothing to do with this family. But I'm very encouraged by the fact she was friendly to me.'

'Perhaps she came to the Fayre especially so she could bump into you?' said Lottie.

Barty's face reddened. 'No, I don't think so. I think she just wanted to come and enjoy the festivities like the rest of us. She told me she particularly liked the grotto, I need to have a look at it. I've heard it's quite a spectacle.'

'It is,' said Lottie. 'Mildred and I visited. But even with all its Christmas lighting, I still find it a little spooky. Mildred was telling me all about the hermit that lived there.'

'Oh yes, Hector the Hermit.'

'That was his name?'

'I believe so. Some great-great-great-grandfather of mine let him live there for a few years.'

'I heard it was fifty years.'

Barty laughed. 'That's what happens when the story gets repeated by a lot of people. I'm sure it was only a few years.'

'Apparently, Hector the Hermit was driven out of the village for cursing some children to death.'

'Goodness me, that's not the story I remember! I heard he had a strange visitation on the road to Oswestry. He claimed to have been visited by an angel. But when he told people the story, they decided he was going mad and laughed at him. Apparently, he couldn't bear the ridicule, so he asked one of my ancestors if he could live in the grotto.'

'And he died there.'

'He died there? I hope not! I heard he then moved to a village near Shrewsbury.'

'So the story isn't as bad as I'd believed,' said Lottie. 'I'm pleased I heard your version, Barty, because now the grotto feels a little less creepy.'

'Even so, surely you both have to admit the story of Hector the Hermit sounds a little strange,' said Mrs Moore. 'He probably didn't exist at all.'

'Help!' came a distant cry.

The carol singers stopped and Lottie heard concerned gasps from around her.

'Oh *help*!'

Stumbling towards them all was a lady in a fur-trimmed coat. She was waving her arms and slipping in the snow.

It was Lily Granger.

'Call a doctor!' she cried. 'Call the police! There's been a murder!'

Chapter Ten

'THESE ARE the facts as we know them,' said Detective Inspector Lloyd as he paced in front of the Christmas tree in the drawing room. He was a short, stocky man with no neck and he puffed on a pipe. 'Mrs Lily Granger arrived at the grotto at twenty minutes to four this afternoon and found the place in darkness. The candles and lanterns for the Christmas display had been extinguished. She discovered Mrs Ruth Campbell lying deceased on the floor. The victim appears to have died from a gunshot wound.'

The mayor gave a loud sob. 'I am bereft!' He slumped in a chair, still dressed in his Father Christmas outfit. 'Utterly bereft! I can't imagine existing without Ruth. The past three years have been the happiest of my life. I had finally found true love. And now someone has taken her away from me! Who did this? When I find them, I shall strangle them until they're—'

The detective held up his pipe to interrupt him. 'I realise you're upset, Mr Campbell, but please don't take matters into your own hands. When we discover who did this, we will arrest them, and they will stand trial and face proper justice.'

'But how are you going to catch them, Detective? There were hundreds of people here this afternoon. Any one of them could have done it!'

'The man's right,' said Lord Buckley-Phipps. 'This could be a complicated case. Are you going to request assistance from Scotland Yard, Detective?'

'Yes, I shall, my lord. Although I hear the railway line between London and Shrewsbury is currently impassable due to snowfall. We may have to wait a few days for help to arrive.'

'Well, it looks like you've got your work cut out,' said Lord Buckley-Phipps.

'Surely someone heard the gunshot?' said Lady Buckley-Phipps.

'I'm hoping we'll find someone who heard it, my lady,' said the detective. 'But nobody has come forward to say so just yet. The grotto is situated some distance from the centre of the Fayre, so it's possible no one heard the shot. What we need to do is establish the time when the attack took place. Did anyone see Mrs Campbell this afternoon?'

'We all did,' said Lord Buckley-Phipps.

'She was ice skating for a while,' said Barty. 'And she knocked Mrs Moore over.'

'Is that so?' said the detective.

'It was an accident,' said Mrs Moore.

'I saw Mrs Campbell after that,' said Lottie. 'Mildred and I had just left the grotto when we saw her walking towards the grotto with a gentleman.'

'Who?' asked the mayor.

'I didn't recognise him. He was tall and fair-haired, smartly dressed, and had a thick overcoat on.'

The detective addressed the room. 'Does anyone recognise Miss Sprigg's description of this man?'

There was muttering and a general shaking of heads.

'Mr Campbell?' asked the detective. 'Do you recognise the man Miss Sprigg describes?'

The mayor shook his head. 'I've no idea who he is at all, Detective. But he must be the man who murdered my wife!'

Chapter Eleven

'BUT WHO IS THIS MAN?' said Lord Buckley-Phipps. 'And why does no one here recognise the description of him?'

'I'll find him, my lord,' said Detective Inspector Lloyd. 'And I think we should be cautious about assuming he's the murderer.'

'My wife is seen with a strange man shortly before her murder and you think he could be innocent?' said the mayor. 'What nonsense!'

'Perhaps Lily Granger saw the stranger,' said Mrs Moore. 'She arrived at the grotto a short while later. She might even know who he is.'

'I shall ask her,' said the detective. 'And I propose to hold a meeting in the village hall tomorrow morning where everybody who attended the Fayre can come along and speak to me and my men. We need to find more witnesses and we also need to find the weapon. It's possible the murderer took the gun with them. It's also possible they've discarded it somewhere in the grounds.'

'What about footprints in the snow?' said Lord Buckley-Phipps. 'Surely the culprit has left their footprints?'

'And so have an awful lot of other people, Ivan,' said his wife. 'I think it will be impossible to trace them.'

'We need to establish who could have wished the mayoress harm,' said the detective. 'Can you think of anybody your wife had fallen out with, Mr Campbell?'

He shook his head. 'No.'

'Lily Granger told me she and Ruth Campbell were both seeking to be elected as chairperson of the Lowton Chorley Ladies' Society,' said Mrs Moore. 'I understand there was some rivalry between them.'

'I shouldn't think the ladies from the local Ladies' Society are going to murder each other,' chuckled Lord Buckley-Phipps.

'You never can tell,' said Mrs Moore. 'These disputes can get very competitive indeed.'

'So, are you suggesting, Roberta, that Mrs Granger could have murdered the mayoress in the grotto?' said Lady Buckley-Phipps.

'I don't think she should be ruled out, Lucinda.'

'I'm not going to pretend my wife and Lily Granger were the best of friends,' said the mayor. 'But I refuse to believe Mrs Granger would have shot her. The rivalry between them would never have led to that.'

'But there was rivalry?' asked the detective. He inhaled on his pipe.

'A little.'

'And Mrs Granger was the one who discovered Mrs Campbell,' said Lord Buckley-Phipps. 'I'm not suggesting she's guilty, but she did have the opportunity to carry out the deed.'

'That would mean she was walking about the Christmas Fayre with a loaded gun on her!' said Lady Buckley-Phipps. 'I refuse to believe it.'

'Well, whoever the culprit was, they were walking about

with a loaded gun on them, Lucinda,' said her husband. 'It's not a nice thought, but we have to accept it.'

'Lottie and I spoke to Lily Granger before she left for the grotto,' said Mrs Moore. 'We had a normal chat, and she didn't seem like someone who had a gun on her and was planning a murder. Had she been preparing herself to do such a thing, I think she would have appeared tense or nervous in some way.'

'A fair point,' said Lord Buckley-Phipps.

Detective Inspector Lloyd blew out a cloud of pipe smoke. 'I shall need to interview you all in turn,' he said. 'May I use the music room for the purpose, my lord?'

'Of course.'

'Thank you.' He turned to the mayor. 'Mr Campbell, I'd like to begin with you if I may.'

'WOULD you like to change your clothes before we begin, Mr Campbell?' asked Detective Inspector Lloyd.

Walter was sitting at a table in the music room next to a piano. He looked down at his red and white costume and sighed. 'I'd forgotten I was wearing this,' he said. 'One moment I was handing out presents to happy children and then... my life has changed forever.'

'Please accept my condolences, Mr Campbell.' The detective opened his notebook. 'I shall try to keep this interview as short as possible.'

'Thank you.' He knew Detective Inspector Lloyd reasonably well and had little confidence in his ability to solve the case. The last time he'd encountered him was when his bicycle had been stolen. Lloyd had neither found the thief nor recovered the bicycle. Police training wasn't what it used to be.

'How long were you and Ruth Campbell married for?'

'Three years. I've said it before, and I'll say it again. They were the happiest three years of my life.'

'And was Ruth your first wife?'

'No, she was my fourth. I knew I truly loved Ruth because

I'd had three failed marriages before her. Sometimes it can take a while to find the perfect lady.'

'When did you last see your wife, Mr Campbell?'

'It was just after I cut the ribbon to open the Fayre. We posed for some photographs for the local press photographer.' He paused to blow his nose loudly into his handkerchief. 'Then I had to get up to the house to put on my costume. Ruth told me she was going to go ice skating and look around the stalls. That was the last time I saw her. She disappeared into the crowd and that was that. If only I had known it would be the last time I saw her! I don't know how life can continue without her.'

'It's a very shocking event indeed. How was your wife's mood when you last saw her?'

'She was excited about the Christmas Fayre. She was looking forward to buying some Christmas gifts from the stalls, and we arranged that I would join her once I'd finished handing out the presents. I was so lucky to be married to such a...' He trailed off and blew his nose into his handkerchief again. 'I'm sorry, Detective, this is terribly difficult.'

The detective gave him a concerned glance, and the mayor felt sure the man was convinced of his unquestionable love for his wife.

'And then I heard the awful news,' he continued. 'I had just visited the bathroom because I had taken a break from handing out presents. And my elf was waiting for me in the corridor. He told me the dreadful news.'

'Your elf?'

'Jack the footman. He was playing the role of my elf. Someone had run up to the house to find me after Lily Granger raised the alarm. I was in the bathroom at the time and poor Jack had to be the bearer of bad news.'

'Do you have any idea who the gentleman was who accompanied your wife to the grotto?'

'None!' It frustrated him that he didn't recognise the description of the man. Who had he been? 'I can only imagine he was a friend who Ruth bumped into at the Fayre. But if you ask me, Detective, I think it's quite clear he's the murderer!'

'Maybe he is. We shall work hard to find him.' The detective took a puff on his pipe. 'I realise this is a difficult question for you to hear at a time like this, Mr Campbell. But was your marriage a happy one?'

The question felt like a blow to the stomach. Walter found himself riled. 'How dare you ask such a thing, Detective! I've just told you how much I loved my wife. How could you possibly question it?'

'Like I said, Mr Campbell, it's a difficult question. But you must understand that it's the sort of question I must ask. After all, no one is above suspicion at this moment in time.'

'You suspect me?'

'No, I don't suspect you, Mr Campbell. But I do need to gather all the facts. If your marriage had been unhappy, for example, then perhaps you would have had a motive for harming your wife.'

'Impossible!' He got to his feet. 'I can't sit here and listen to such nonsense while I'm a grieving widower! My wife has just been murdered, and you're sitting here accusing me of committing the crime!'

'I'm not accusing you, Mr Campbell. I'm merely inquiring about the happiness of your marriage.'

'It was perfectly happy! I've already told you that Ruth was the love of my life. I'm sorry, but I don't think I can answer any more of your questions. This is too upsetting.'

He sank into his chair again, weak with grief.

'Very well, Mr Campbell. You have my greatest sympathy at this time.'

'Sympathy? It doesn't feel like sympathy when you're asking me questions like that.'

'I have to ask everyone searching questions, I'm afraid. It's the only way I can get to the bottom of this mystery. But please go and get some rest somewhere. I shall probably need to speak to you again tomorrow.'

'I don't know why. I haven't got anything more I can tell you.'

'Something may come up from my other interviews which I need to ask you about.'

'I see.' He couldn't believe the detective had asked him such a personal question about his marriage. The cheek of the man!

'Please could you ask Mrs Moore and Miss Sprigg to see me now?' asked the detective.

'You want me to be your messenger?'

'It's helpful if each person fetches the next for me. It saves me time and I'm sure you'd want me to spend my time wisely, Mr Campbell.'

'Of course.' He gave a sniff and hoped Lloyd had believed everything he'd told him.

Chapter Thirteen

LOTTIE AND MRS MOORE sat in the music room facing Detective Inspector Lloyd. He was familiar to the pair of them, having worked on the case of Percy Abercromby a few months previously.

It was dark outside now, and the heavy brocade curtains had been drawn. Rosie warmed herself in front of the fire.

'So Ruth Campbell knocked you over when you were skating on the lake, Mrs Moore,' said the detective.

'Oh, that. It was nothing, really. She just brushed against me, but because I wasn't very steady on my skates, I tumbled over. It was an accident.'

'You seem to be making light of the event, Mrs Moore. And yet I have heard from a few witnesses that you took quite a tumble.'

'I did. That's because I was on ice skates. But I'm making light of it because it was an accident. I hope you're not going to think that I was so offended by the incident that I decided to take my revenge on Mrs Campbell by murdering her in the grotto.'

'No, no,' the detective sat back in his chair. 'That would be quite preposterous.'

'Yes, it would. And don't forget, Detective, that Miss Sprigg here is very good at solving cases like this.'

Detective Inspector Lloyd looked at Lottie through narrowed eyes. 'I can't deny you did a good job of solving the last case, Miss Sprigg. But this case will be in the hands of a detective from Scotland Yard as soon as the trains can get through from London. So I really don't advise doing any investigating with this one. Not unless you want to come up against Scotland Yard.'

'I think Lottie is as clever as any Scotland Yard detective,' said Mrs Moore.

'No, I'm not,' said Lottie, embarrassed to be talked about in this way.

'Perhaps one day in the future, Scotland Yard will employ ladies,' said the detective. 'But I should think that will be a very long time in the future indeed. Now, let's return to the matter at hand. When did you last see Ruth Campbell, Mrs Moore?'

'On the lake. And after my tumble, I took myself off for a nice mug of hot chocolate.'

'So you didn't see Mrs Campbell again after that?'

'No, I didn't.'

The detective turned to Lottie. 'And Miss Sprigg. You saw Mrs Campbell with the fair-haired man.'

'Yes, that's right.'

'Can you tell me more about the pair as you passed them? Were they talking about something? Laughing? Arguing?'

'I didn't pay them much attention,' said Lottie. 'I smiled at Mrs Campbell as she passed, but she just acknowledged me with a quick glance. She seemed to be listening to something the gentleman was saying, so the mood between them was fairly serious. But I didn't get the impression they had fallen out. There was nothing about them that aroused my suspicion, but I did wonder who he was.'

'I'm quite confident that we'll determine his identity soon enough,' said the detective. 'But it is odd that the man hasn't volunteered himself as a witness yet. He clearly has some useful information, but he hasn't come forward.'

'And if he's the murderer, then I doubt he's going to,' said Mrs Moore. 'You need to find him soon, Detective. If he's the culprit, he could cause a lot more trouble.'

Chapter Fourteen

'Oh dear, look at this news story,' said Mrs Moore at the breakfast table the following morning. She held up a copy of the local newspaper with the headline *The Grotto Curse Strikes Again*. 'It's quite ridiculous, isn't it?' she continued. 'You should read what the local people have been saying about it. There's a tall tale about Hector the Hermit, who was chased out of the village and hid in the grotto for fifty years until he died there.'

'Most of that story is untrue, Roberta,' said Lord Buckley-Phipps. 'Apparently, a man did live in the grotto, but only for a few years.'

'It says here that locals have long believed that the grotto has been cursed and haunted by evil spirits. Apparently, twelve years ago, a gardener on the Fortescue Manor estate died of fright after hearing a howling noise from the grotto.'

'Rubbish.'

'And how do they know he heard a howling noise if he died of fright? Presumably, he was dead and unable to tell them what had caused it. Isn't it nonsense how no one ever questions these tales? It also says in this article that Hector the Hermit caused livestock to die and poisoned the water supply.'

'This is the trouble with simple-minded people,' said Lord Buckley-Phipps. 'They're unable to separate fact from fiction. And these stories were invented in the old days, when there wasn't a great deal going on outside of the daily toil. Back then, people sat by the fire and made up ridiculous tales.'

'I realise most of the stories are probably untrue,' said Lottie. 'But they're quite creepy, aren't they?'

'They are, which is exactly why they're popular,' said Mrs Moore. 'People enjoy being scared. Someone in this newspaper article says he believes Ruth Campbell was murdered in the grotto by a ghost.'

'Well, the chap needs his head examined,' said Lord Buckley-Phipps. 'And shame on the local rag for printing such rubbish. I hope Detective Inspector Lloyd finds that gentleman today.'

'The one who Lottie saw walking with Mrs Campbell?'

'Exactly. When someone's arrested for the murder, the silly nonsense will stop. And it can't happen soon enough, as far as I'm concerned.'

Chapter Fifteen

'Do you mind if I smoke, Detective?'

'Not at all.'

Lily Granger wondered why she'd asked permission when he was sitting opposite her puffing on his pipe. She placed a cigarette in her silver cigarette holder and lit it.

She puffed out a plume of smoke and glanced around the music room of Fortescue Manor. This was the first time she'd been in the house and she envied the splendour the Buckley-Phipps family lived in. There was a piano to her right and a harp to her left. She and Detective Inspector Lloyd sat on red and gold upholstered chairs at a circular table. A clock ticked noisily on the mantelpiece. 'I still can't believe this has happened,' she said. 'Poor Ruth.'

'When did you last see Mrs Campbell?'

'Alive, you mean?'

'Yes. When did you last see your friend alive?'

'Well, I wouldn't really describe her as a friend.'

'How would you describe her?'

'As an acquaintance.'

'When did you last see your acquaintance, Mrs Campbell, alive?'

'I think it must have been when she was ice skating on the frozen lake. And she knocked over Lady Buckley-Phipps's sister.'

'Mrs Moore?'

'That's right.'

'And when did you last speak to Mrs Campbell?'

'I spoke to her briefly by the gingerbread stall yesterday.'

'And what did you discuss?'

'It was rather perfunctory. I commented on what a lovely afternoon it was and how the fresh snowfall had created a wonderful backdrop for the Christmas Fayre.'

This wasn't what the conversation had been about at all. She could feel the anger rising within her as she recalled how Ruth Campbell had accused her of rigging the vote for the chairperson.

'Then she went off to hobnob with some dignitaries,' said Lily. 'She considered herself quite important when her husband became mayor.'

'Was one of the dignitaries a tall, fair-haired man? Smartly dressed and wearing a thick overcoat?'

'I don't know, I didn't see him.'

'Do you recognise the man from my description of him?'

'I'm afraid not, Detective.'

'He was seen walking with Mrs Campbell to the grotto. You can't have been too far behind them.'

'I didn't see them.'

'Perhaps you saw the gentleman walking back from the grotto?'

'No. Is he the murderer?'

'I don't know yet.'

The detective sat back in his chair and puffed on his pipe.

'I get the impression from you, Mrs Granger, that you bore Ruth Campbell some resentment.'

She startled at this. 'Oh no, Detective, you've got that completely wrong. I'm sorry if I appear a little jaded, I'm just in shock still. You never expect to find someone lying on the floor like that. Dead.'

The detective nodded. 'I understand. It must have been extremely upsetting. I hear both you and Ruth Campbell were in contention for the position of chair of the Lowton Chorley Ladies' Society.'

It hadn't taken long for their feud to become public knowledge. She forced a smile. 'Yes, that's right, Detective. We've both been members for some time. The current chair is stepping down due to old age, and we both put our names forward to replace her.'

'And did that create animosity between you?'

'Oh no! Although we were rivals for the position of chair, it didn't cause any problems between us.' She gave a laugh to demonstrate how unlikely this could have been. 'We were both very sensible and mature about it. It's a fact of life, isn't it, Detective? Sometimes there is some competition between people. But it doesn't have to spill over into bitterness or even revenge. I always said to Ruth, "May the best woman win."' She gave a laugh again to show how she could turn the situation into something humorous. 'That was the attitude we both had.'

'So what stage had the bid for chair reached?'

'The Ladies' Society had voted, and we'd both received an equal number of votes.'

'So how was it to be finally decided between you?'

'It was quite simple. We were going to put it to another vote.'

'And if that result had also tied? Then what would have happened?'

'The plan was to call upon the residents of Lowton Chorley to vote, too.'

'I realise it's probably too early to know the answer to this, but what do you think will happen now that Mrs Campbell is no longer in the running?'

'I expect it will fall to me to become the chair. It will be difficult to take on the responsibility given the circumstances, but I'm prepared to step up and do what is right.'

'That's very noble of you, Mrs Granger.'

'Thank you. I like to think so.'

'Can you tell me why you chose to visit the grotto when you did?'

'Because I'd heard from other people that it was very pretty.'

'You didn't go there because you knew Ruth Campbell would be there?'

'No! How would I even have known she was there?'

'Perhaps you saw her walk off in that direction?'

'No, I didn't. I didn't know she was there, and I certainly didn't expect to find the place in darkness. The murderer clearly wanted to cover up what they'd just done.'

'And, just to be clear, you didn't see anyone heading in the opposite direction? Someone who could have just left the grotto?'

'No. I didn't see that fair-haired man or anyone else. It was eerily quiet near the grotto. It gives me the shivers just thinking about it. And to find it in darkness like that...' She clasped a hand to her chest to show how affected she'd felt by it. 'Just awful,' she added in a choked voice.

'Can you think of anybody who would have wished to harm Ruth Campbell?'

'I'm afraid I can.'

'Who?'

'I can't name specific names, Detective, because there are

too many to mention. But she had an imperious manner which rubbed many people up the wrong way. And when she assumed the title of mayoress, she got very self-important about it. It's important to remember she was only mayoress because her husband had become mayor. She'd done nothing to achieve the role on her own merit. And yet she acted as though she had.' She shook her head sadly. 'I feel so awful talking about her in this way, but facts are facts, Detective. Ruth Campbell was not well liked.'

Chapter Sixteen

AFTER BREAKFAST, Lottie found Mildred dusting the ornaments in the library.

'What did the detective ask you last night?' asked the maid.

'He just wanted to know when Mrs Moore and I had last seen Ruth Campbell. And he asked about the man you and I saw her with.'

'No one knows who he is yet?'

'Not yet.'

'I don't understand it. Everyone seems to know everyone else in Lowton Chorley, apart from him. He has to be the murderer, doesn't he? Although he didn't look like one.'

'What does a murderer look like?'

'I don't know.' Mildred examined her feather duster as she thought. 'Scary looking maybe?' Then she laughed. 'You can't tell a murderer when you see one, can you?'

'Not really.'

'I've been given the afternoon off,' said Mildred. 'But it's not really time off. My mother needs help at the laundry. She's got two people off with sickness and she's asked Miss Hudson if she can spare me for a few hours to help. Me and my brothers and sisters are going to take turns down there.' Mildred's mother had run the laundry in Lowton Chorley for several years.

'I can help too,' said Lottie.

Mildred laughed. 'No, Lottie! You're too important these days to be helping with laundry.'

'Of course I'm not! I'm no more important than when I was a maid here. And I think Rosie will enjoy it too. I'll check if Mrs Moore needs me for anything this afternoon, but I'm sure she won't mind me joining you.'

Helping at the laundry would give Lottie the opportunity to speak to Mildred's mother. She'd described Ruth Campbell as a local busybody, and Lottie hoped she'd learn a little more from her about the mayoress.

That afternoon, Lottie, Rosie and Mildred walked down to the village. The white fields were bright in the sunlight, and the hedgerows and trees along the lane were frosted with snow. A robin watched them from a frozen hawthorn branch. Its red breast was easy to spot in the white surroundings.

Lowton Chorley laundry was situated on the high street. Snow had been swept from the cobbles and the shop windows were filled with colourful Christmas displays.

Inside the laundry, the air was steamy and smelled of soap. Mildred's mother stood behind a small counter sorting some paperwork. Behind her was the door which led to the washing tubs, mangles and drying racks.

'Hello Mildred, you've brought Lottie with you too!' Mrs Mallet resembled her daughter with a freckled face and chubby arms. Her red hair was pinned back and had streaks of grey. 'I hear you're a young lady now, Lottie,' she added with a smile.

'No, not a lady. I've been travelling with my employer, Mrs Moore.'

'Mildred's told me all about it. You've seen the pyramids and the Eiffel Tower, and you've travelled along the canals in Venice. What an amazing thing to do!' Rosie walked over to Mrs Mallet and wagged her tail as she was patted on the head.

'Lottie's come to help as well, Mother,' said Mildred.

'Well, that's very kind of you, Lottie. Are you sure you know what you're letting yourself in for?'

'I think so.'

'If you're both working here, that will give me the chance to put on the kettle and make some tea for us all.' She gestured at the door behind her. 'Mrs Simons has just brought in a large bag and says she needs it as soon as possible. I was tempted to tell her she should have brought it in earlier, but I kept my mouth shut. So her laundry needs to go in and we've got a lot that needs hanging up to dry.'

Lottie and Mildred put on aprons and rolled up their sleeves. Then Lottie loaded a washing tub with Mrs Simons' laundry while Mildred hung damp laundry on a drying rack.

Mrs Mallet brought in three mugs of tea.

'It's a shame the Christmas Fayre was ruined by that murder,' she said, handing Lottie a mug. 'We were having a lovely time until someone chose to ruin it.'

'Did you know Mrs Campbell well?' Lottie asked her.

'Not very well. She came in here once or twice but it was her housekeeper who usually brought in the laundry. I've heard she liked to look down on people.'

'Mrs Campbell or the housekeeper?' asked Mildred.

'Mrs Campbell, you silly billy. But the housekeeper was snooty too. And apparently Mrs Campbell got even worse when she became mayoress. She thought she was the most important lady in the village. And Oswestry too.' She sighed. 'These people usually get their comeuppance one way or another, don't they? I'm sad she died, she didn't deserve that. But I'm a big believer in things coming back to haunt you.'

'I wonder who the murderer was,' said Lottie.

'It wouldn't surprise me if the cook did it,' said Mrs Mallet.

'Mrs Palmer?'

'Yes, that's the one.'

'Why?'

'Because Mrs Campbell dismissed her from her job. Apparently, she told Mrs Palmer she was dreadful at cooking and should seek out another profession.'

'That's not a nice thing to say.'

'It isn't, is it? Anyway, that was a few months ago. And then Mrs Palmer went to work at Fortescue Manor.'

'Miss Hudson, the housekeeper, must have known Mrs Palmer had worked for Mrs Campbell because she would have had to ask for a character reference.'

'Maybe,' said Mrs Mallet.

'I can't believe Mrs Palmer could have murdered Mrs Campbell,' said Mildred.

'Neither can I,' said her mother. 'But she had a reason to.'

'You'd have thought Mrs Palmer would have been too tired from baking all those mince pies to plan a murder,' said Mildred. 'And someone would have seen her going to or from the grotto. And where would she have got the gun from?'

'The gun room?' said her mother.

'Lord Buckley-Phipps had it checked,' said Mildred. 'There are no guns missing.'

'Well, it's a mystery,' said Mrs Mallet. 'All I'm saying is what I heard.'

'I wonder where the gun is now?' said Lottie. 'If Mrs

Palmer committed the murder, then she could have hidden the weapon somewhere in the house.'

'Or in her house,' said Mrs Mallet. 'She lives on the estate with her husband, doesn't she? He's been a labourer at Fortescue Manor for some years.'

'I'm struggling to believe Mrs Palmer could have done such a thing,' said Lottie. 'I don't know her very well, but I don't think she could be a murderer.'

'But you've thought this sort of thing before, haven't you, Lottie?' said Mildred. 'And you know yourself that sometimes the most surprising people can do such awful things.'

'Well, if it is Mrs Palmer, how can we find some evidence? I suppose we could try to find out where she was at the time of Mrs Campbell's murder. If she has an alibi, then she can be ruled out.'

'We could ask the staff, couldn't we?' said Mildred.

'But we need to be careful. If Mrs Palmer hears we suspect her, she's not going to be happy about it.'

'Yes, you need to be careful,' said Mrs Mallet. 'I've heard Mrs Palmer has a short temper. She's not the sort of lady you want to get on the wrong side of.'

Chapter Seventeen

WALTER CAMPBELL WAS WARMING his feet by the fire when his housekeeper entered the sitting room.

'Miss Roberts is here, sir. What shall I tell her?'

'Miss Roberts?'

'Yes. Annie Roberts.'

'Oh.' It was risky of her to visit him so soon after Ruth's death. 'Did she say what she wanted?'

'No. I can only imagine she's here to express her condolences.'

'Alright then.' He pushed his feet into his leather slippers and got out of his seat. 'Show her in, please.'

Annie stepped into the room. She wore a dark grey woollen dress and a smart black cloche hat was pulled over her bright blonde hair. She closed the door behind her and dashed over to him. 'Oh Walter! How are you?'

'Fine,' he whispered. 'But keep your voice down. What are you doing here?'

'I came to see how you are!'

'How do you think I am?'

'I don't know!'

'Oh, sit down over there.' He directed her to a chair far away from his. 'I don't want the housekeeper getting suspicious about us. You could have waited a little longer until you called on me. I should only be receiving family and close friends at the moment.'

'Don't you consider me one of them?' Her voice was sulky, and she pushed her lower lip out.

'Yes, but no one's supposed to know, are they?'

'Alright then. I won't stay for long. Have the police caught the culprit yet?'

'Of course not. And I thought Detective Inspector Lloyd would show me some sympathy. But instead he asked me how happy my marriage was!'

'So what did you say?'

'I told him how much I loved Ruth and cared about her and all the rest of it.'

Annie sighed. 'Oh.'

'I lied, obviously. But detectives are trained to spot lies, so it all felt a bit uncomfortable. I suppose I did love and care about her once. So it wasn't a completely outrageous lie that I told him. It was a half-truth.'

Annie's eyes narrowed. 'So does that mean you half-loved her?'

'Oh dear, I can tell I'm getting into hot water now. Of course, my marriage to Ruth wasn't happy, because I found you, Annie. But I don't want the detective to know that, do I? If I tell him the truth, then he's going to suspect me, isn't he? So I have to play the part of a grieving widower. Surely you understand that?'

'Yes, I understand that. But you must understand too that it's rather hurtful for me to hear you half-loved her.'

He gritted his teeth. The very last thing he wanted was an argument. 'I loved her when I married her, Annie. I should think that's quite obvious, isn't it? Then things quickly turned

63

sour. You know how it is. You're the woman I love, and you must believe it. But please appreciate I have to act the part at the moment. I can't have people pointing fingers at me. And I'm quite sure you don't want people pointing fingers at me either.'

'How are you going to stop people from finding out about our affair? The detective is only going to keep asking questions.'

'I can handle Detective Inspector Lloyd. And besides, I'm the mayor! I'm more important than he is. If he oversteps the mark, then I shall have a word with his superiors.'

'But you won't be mayor forever, Walter, and in the eyes of the law, all men are equal. If he suspects you, then he's going to keep asking you questions. Detectives are experienced in these matters. Most people lie to them, and they know what they're looking for.'

Walter felt an uncomfortable shift in his stomach. Annie was right. He was doing his best to play the role of a grieving widower, but even a detective like Detective Inspector Lloyd could see through it.

'Well, we just have to do our best. We've kept this affair secret so far, and we must continue to do so. Just imagine how upset Ruth's family and friends would be if they knew about it! For their sake, we need to keep it quiet.'

'And what should I say if the detective interviews me?'

'He won't.'

'How do you know that, Walter? He might.'

'Then you must deny everything.'

'I'm hopeless at lying.'

His fingers dug into the arm rests of his chair. 'You can't tell him the truth!'

'I'll try not to. But I feel like he's going to see through me. Our affair is going to be discovered sooner or later, Walter, I just know it!'

'You and I are the only two people who know about it. And we've done a very good job of keeping it top secret.'

'And what about the person who saw us?'

'We don't need to worry about them.'

'How do you know that?'

'Because they would have said something sooner.'

'But now your wife's been murdered, they might recall the time they saw us together. They might assume we hatched a plan to get rid of her.'

'Oh, stop it, Annie! I can't cope with such thoughts at the moment. I think that's extremely unlikely, don't you?'

'No, I don't, Walter. I'm getting very worried.'

She pulled out a handkerchief and began to cry.

Chapter Eighteen

BACK AT FORTESCUE MANOR, Lottie and Rosie visited Mrs Moore's room as she was getting ready for dinner. She sat at her dressing table, powdering her face.

'Mrs Palmer, the cook, used to work for the mayor and mayoress?' she said once Lottie had told her what she'd learned from Mildred's mother. 'How interesting. I wonder if Miss Hudson knew. Let's ask her.'

She rang the servant bell, and Nelly came to the door a moment later. 'Please could you fetch Miss Hudson for me, Nelly?' asked Mrs Moore.

'Of course, madam.'

'I don't want to make any trouble for Mrs Palmer,' said Lottie, recalling Mrs Mallet's warning that the cook had a short temper.

'I realise that. We'll make it clear to Miss Hudson that this is a discreet conversation.'

'Mrs Palmer has never mentioned she used to work for Mr and Mrs Campbell,' said Miss Hudson a short while later. She stood close to the door. A tall, sombre figure in her dark dress.

'Presumably it's because the employment didn't end well,' said Mrs Moore. 'Apparently, Mrs Campbell dismissed her from her job.'

'May I ask where you heard this?'

'Lottie heard it in the laundry.'

'Village gossip,' said the housekeeper with a sniff. 'I expect there's a lot of it about at the moment.'

'There probably is,' said Mrs Moore. 'But I don't see why someone would make it up. And besides, it's easily proven. Presumably, Mrs Palmer didn't list Mrs Campbell as a reference when she was employed here.'

'No, she didn't. The person I contacted for a reference was Mrs Watson. In fact, come to think of it, there was a recent two-month gap in Mrs Palmer's employment. She told me she'd had some family business to attend to, and that was why she hadn't worked for a couple of months. But I suppose it could have been the time she took up her ill-fated position with Mrs Campbell. Do you know the exact nature of Mrs Campbell's complaint?'

'Apparently, she told Mrs Palmer she was dreadful at cooking and should seek out another profession,' said Lottie.

'Really? Well, Mrs Campbell was known for her sharp tongue. If that's what she said, then I think it's a little unreasonable. Her ladyship and I have been quite content with Mrs Palmer's work here. I will ask Mrs Palmer if the rumours are true.'

'You won't mention my name when you speak to her, will you, Miss Hudson?' said Mrs Moore. 'Or Lottie's name, for that matter. We don't wish Mrs Palmer to know we've been discussing her behind her back. I don't think she'd take too kindly to that.'

'No, I don't think she would. I shall ask about it merely because she should have honestly disclosed her previous employment.'

'You're not going to scold her, are you?'

'No. Like I say, she does a good job. We don't want to lose her. It's difficult to find good staff these days.' The housekeeper turned to leave, then stopped again. 'You don't think she...?'

'She what?' said Mrs Moore.

'The murder. Do you suspect her?'

'Oh no! I'm sure the cook would never have done such a thing.'

'No. She wouldn't have.'

Chapter Nineteen

LILY GRANGER PULLED out the little mirror from her handbag and held it up as she applied a fresh layer of red lipstick. She'd been the first to arrive at the village hall that evening and had arranged the chairs neatly in front of the stage.

The emergency meeting of the Lowton Chorley Ladies' Society was due to start in fifteen minutes. After examining her face in her mirror, Lily smoothed her black dress then went over to the Christmas tree in the corner and rearranged some decorations as she waited.

A gust of chilly wind from the door announced the arrival of the first attendee. The rest were quick to follow, all dressed in black and speaking in hushed, reverent tones.

At half-past seven, Lily climbed the wooden steps to the stage and cleared her throat. This was her moment.

'Thank you, everyone, for coming here this evening at such short notice.' She enjoyed the way her voice rang out across the hall. 'I'm sure I speak for everyone here when I say how completely and utterly devastated we all are by Ruth Campbell's untimely passing. She was a dedicated and devoted member of the Lowton Chorley Ladies' Society and I, for one, will miss her enormously. We all will. And to find her in the grotto like I did...' She placed her hand on her mouth as if grief had choked her words. Then she made a show of composing herself as she prepared to continue. A few sniffs emanated from the audience.

'I have extended my condolences on behalf of the Ladies' Society to Mr Campbell, who, I'm sure you know, is extremely upset by what has happened to his beloved Ruth. She was a respected and highly regarded lady, and I was incredibly surprised to receive the same number of votes as her in the election for chair. She should have won the vote, and she should have been the one standing here in front of you this evening. She would have made an excellent chairlady, but sadly that will never be.'

Lily paused for another show of emotion, then continued.

'I don't think any of us can pretend the past few months have been easy. The resignation of our previous chair has left the Ladies' Society rudderless, and it's been far from plain sailing as we've struggled to navigate the choppy waters of choosing a new chair.' She glanced at the faces in the audience, hoping they'd been impressed with her boat analogy. The faces remained impassive, so she continued. 'But I believe we have sighted dry land ahead! I reassure you all now that I intend to steer the Lowton Chorley Ladies' Society into calmer waters. I will lead with conviction and dedication and transform our group into a society we can be proud of! My first proposal is a memorial to the late Ruth Campbell. We can have a discussion about what form we think this should take. Perhaps it can be a plaque, a bench, or even a small statue? What do people think?'

A blonde lady in a black cloche hat raised her hand. 'Yes, Annie Roberts?'

'Have you just made yourself the chair of the Ladies' Society?'

'Yes, I have. With Ruth Campbell no longer with us, only one candidate remains.'

'But only half of us voted for you. The other half voted for Ruth.'

'Agreed. The plan was to hold another vote, wasn't it? But that can't happen now because Ruth is no longer with us.'

'In the event that a candidate can no longer stand, because she has died, then another candidate should be allowed to stand in her place,' said Annie.

Lily felt her heart sink. She had waited for this proud moment for years. As she'd watched the previous chair age, then step down from her duties, she had grown confident that she would be the replacement. Ruth Campbell had tried to thwart her, but she was gone now. Ever since Ruth's death, Lily had felt sure the position of chair was hers. And now she was being questioned by Annie Roberts!

'Annie's right,' said Olivia Lawson. 'I think it's only fair that the contest begins again. If you had won the majority of the votes, then, of course, we would accept you as our chair. But the Ladies' Society was divided right down the middle. You don't actually have the backing of half the Ladies' Society.'

Lily felt her heart pound with anger. She forced a smile. 'I think to start the contest all over again would be very damaging for the Ladies' Society. Like I said, we've been in choppy waters for the past few months. I think we'll suffer more damage if we try to weather the storm any longer. I stand before you now, offering to lead us out of the turmoil. Surely you don't want to delay that by restarting the contest. And besides, I'm not aware any of you actually wish to be chair, do you?'

'I think a few people would like to give it a go,' said Annie.

'The reason we didn't put our names forward before is because it was such a fierce competition between you and Ruth. But with Ruth no longer here, there's an opportunity for someone else to try their luck.'

Lily sighed. Annie was a nuisance. 'We really don't want to be doing this all over again,' she said. 'We've all been through a distressing time and I think the least we can do now is accept me as the chair. We've been bogged down in uncertainty for too long. I think it would be disastrous if we continue to prolong it.'

'That's just your opinion,' said Annie. 'But I don't think we can have a leader who hasn't been supported by over half the members of the group. Why don't we put it to a vote?' She glanced around the room. 'Everyone who thinks we should start the leadership contest again, raise your hand.'

Lily's shoulders slumped as most members of the audience raised their hands. 'This isn't a proper vote, Annie,' she said. 'If we're going to hold a vote, a week's notice is required, and it needs to be tabled as an agenda item. I can't accept the validity of this vote.'

'We could do that,' said Annie. 'But it would waste even more time, wouldn't it? I think it's best to accept the results of the informal poll I held just a moment ago and start the contest again.'

Chapter Twenty

'THAT'S A NICE CHRISTMAS CARD, BARTY,' said Mrs Moore. Barty had just opened his post at the breakfast table.

'It is rather, isn't it?' The card depicted two people in a horse-drawn sleigh in a winter wonderland.

'Who's it from?'

Barty's face coloured. 'It's from Evelyn,' he said quietly. He gave his father a sidelong glance.

'How lovely,' said Mrs Moore.

'Evelyn Abercromby?' Lord Buckley-Phipps paused from eating his boiled egg. 'As in our avowed enemy, the Abercromby family?'

'Yes, Father.'

'What's she doing sending you a Christmas card?'

'I think she's being Christmassy, Father.'

'Why?'

'Barty and Evelyn bumped into each other at the Christmas Fayre,' said Mrs Moore.

'Did you?' said Lord Buckley-Phipps. 'Evelyn Abercromby set foot here?'

'Yes, Father. Just for a short while. And we had a pleasant conversation.'

'Did you indeed? Well, you'd better be careful, Barty. She could have been sent here as an agent of her father.'

'Lord Abercromby didn't know she was here.'

'Well, all the same, just be careful.' He wagged a silver spoon at him. 'The Abercrombys can't be trusted.'

'Oh Ivan, it's only a Christmas card,' said Mrs Moore. 'I think it's very touching.'

The butler entered the room. 'Mr Palmer is here to have a word, my lord.'

'But I'm eating breakfast!'

'He says it's quite urgent, my lord.'

'Very well.' Lord Buckley-Phipps pulled his serviette from his collar, placed it on the table, and left the room with the butler.

'I'd like to go to the library today,' Lottie said to Mrs Moore. 'I have some books to return.'

'Can the bus get through to Oswestry at the moment?'

'I heard the road was clear yesterday,' said Barty. 'And I don't think there was any snowfall overnight.'

'Then you should be fine, Lottie,' said Mrs Moore. 'I would come with you but I'm quite happy to stay here to be honest with you.'

Miss Hudson the housekeeper entered the room. 'Mrs Moore,' she said. 'And Miss Sprigg. You'll be interested to know that I spoke to the person we discussed yesterday.'

'Which person?' said Mrs Moore.

'The, erm...' She gave Barty a look, clearly wondering if it was alright for him to overhear.

'Oh, I remember!' said Mrs Moore. 'Mrs Palmer.'

'Yes. She has confirmed that she did indeed once work for—'

'So it's true?'

'Yes. She told me she hadn't mentioned it because she felt ashamed of being dismissed.'

'Who was dismissed?' said Barty.

The housekeeper sighed. 'You know I'm not one for gossip, sir. And I suppose this will become common knowledge before long. Mrs Palmer was once employed by Mr and Mrs Campbell. But she was dismissed from her job by the mayoress who told her she should seek out another profession.'

'How jolly unkind,' said Barty.

'Yes, it is.'

Lord Buckley-Phipps returned to the room. 'Well, that turned out to be quite interesting,' he said as he tucked his serviette back into his collar. 'I just spoke with Mr Palmer. He's been a labourer on this estate for some time and he and his wife occupy a house here. In fact, his wife is the new cook, isn't she? He wanted to let me know he had to report something to the police this morning.'

'What?' said Mrs Moore.

'He's discovered a gun is missing from his house. A pistol, apparently. He last saw it a week ago and can't be sure exactly when it was taken. He's looked high and low, but there's no sign of it anywhere.'

Chapter Twenty-One

LOTTIE FOUND Mildred dusting in the drawing room and told her the news about Mr Palmer's missing gun.

The maid's eyes grew wide. 'She did it, didn't she?' she whispered. 'Mrs Palmer! She's the murderer!'

'I don't know. But it seems suspicious.'

'I think she's really suspicious. I saw her in the corridor first thing this morning and she had a bag in her hand. But when she saw me, she turned around and went the other way.'

'Really? That is strange,' said Lottie. 'Did you see her at the Christmas Fayre?'

Mildred shook her head. 'I don't think so.'

'We need to find out where she was when Mrs Campbell was murdered. If she has an alibi, then we can rule her out.'

'I'll ask the staff if any of them saw her. But I'll do it carefully. But if she's the murderer, then what about the man we saw walking to the grotto with Mrs Campbell?'

'That's a good point. He would have witnessed something, wouldn't he? I wonder when the detective is going to find out who he is. It can't be difficult, can it? Where did he get to after Mrs Campbell was attacked?'

'Perhaps he was so frightened by what he saw that he ran away?' said Mildred.

'But why didn't he raise the alarm?'

'Because he was afraid of the murderer turning on him, too? And perhaps he's still afraid of the murderer? And that's why he's not making himself known.'

'Or perhaps he's the murderer,' said Lottie.

'Then how did he get hold of Mr Palmer's gun?'

'We can't be sure that it was Mr Palmer's gun which was used in the attack,' said Lottie. 'It might just be a coincidence that his gun is missing. But it's a strange coincidence, isn't it? I think both the fair-haired man and Mrs Palmer have to be suspects.'

Chapter Twenty-Two

THE BUS to Oswestry wound through the picturesque Shropshire lanes. Snow covered the rolling hills and the sky was a brilliant blue. Lottie gazed out of the window with Rosie on her lap. Her bag of library books rested on the seat next to her.

She was a regular visitor to Oswestry Library. And not just because she loved books.

Lottie had grown up in the orphanage in the town. She had spoken with her former schoolmistress at the orphanage, Miss Beaufort, a few times since she and Mrs Moore had returned from their summer travels. Lottie hoped to find information about her parents, but Miss Spencer, the owner of the orphanage, was reluctant to reunite children with their parents. Miss Beaufort disagreed with this approach. She'd told Lottie that a lady had visited the orphanage and inquired about her while she was away on her travels. Miss Spencer had told the woman that Lottie hadn't wanted to be contacted by her, something she apparently told everyone who inquired about adopted children at the orphanage.

Miss Beaufort felt sure that Lottie would be able to trace

one or both of her parents, but Lottie had little information to help her. The woman who'd inquired about her had not left her name and had left no clues about her identity. Miss Beaufort had told her that the lady had been in her late thirties and had brown hair and a local accent. She'd been smartly dressed but hadn't appeared to be wealthy. Miss Beaufort said it had been a rainy day, and the woman's overcoat and umbrella were wet, suggesting she'd walked to the orphanage. The fact she'd walked and had a local accent made Lottie feel sure she didn't live far from Oswestry.

The woman had carried a basket and mentioned that she'd just visited the town library. Miss Beaufort had caught sight of a book in the basket and described it as a book of detective stories. This piece of information had made Lottie's heart skip. She loved detective stories. Could the woman who'd enquired about her really be her mother?

Ever since Miss Beaufort had described the woman to Lottie, she had looked out for her in Lowton Chorley and Oswestry. Sometimes she saw a lady who fitted the description but she could never be certain it was the lady she sought.

Lottie had asked Miss Roberts, the librarian, about the woman but she didn't recognise the description. All Lottie felt she could do now was visit the library and hope to see her.

Chapter Twenty-Three

ROSIE COULDN'T ENTER the library, so she waited on the steps outside while Lottie went in. As it was a cold day, Lottie knew she would have to make her visit quick so Rosie wouldn't be sitting in the snow for too long.

Inside, the library was warm and cosy. A fire burned in the grate and a colourful Christmas tree stood by the children's section. There was no sign of the librarian, Miss Roberts, so Lottie placed her returned books on the desk and went over to the shelves for the detective stories.

Since Lottie's return from her travels, she had read through nearly all the detective stories in the library. She could only hope her favourite authors were busy writing some new ones. Then she came across a book she hadn't yet read. She pulled it out and began leafing through it.

As she did so, she could hear two people talking in hushed tones nearby. They were trying to be quiet, but she could just make out what they were saying.

'I refused to let her assume the role of the chair.' Lottie recognised the librarian's voice. 'So I encouraged everyone to raise their hands in favour of the vote being held again.'

'Good for you, Annie,' said a man's voice. 'Who does she think she is? As soon as my wife has died, she tries to take advantage of the situation. That woman is nothing but trouble,' he continued. 'Ruth never liked her.'

Ruth! Did the man's voice belong to the mayor?

'None of us wanted her to become chair,' said Miss Roberts. 'I don't know how she managed to get all those votes. Anyway, I've decided I'm going to stand for chair now and I can only hope I get most of the votes.'

'What a wonderful idea, Annie! I'm sure you will.'

'But that's enough talk about that, Walter. With everything that's happened, do you think we'll be able to spend Christmas together?'

'Oh, I don't know about that. I shall have to wait and see.'

'But it will be the first Christmas where it's just you and me. Isn't that what we always wanted?'

Lottie felt her mouth gaping. Miss Roberts, the librarian, and Mr Campbell, the mayor, were clearly friendly.

'Yes, Annie, it is what we wanted. But what will people say when it's so soon after Ruth's death? How can we explain it to them? I think it's going to be too difficult.'

'But, Walter, you promised we would spend Christmas together. Just the two of us.'

'Yes, and we will do. I just don't think it will be this Christmas. It's all too recent. Can't you see?'

'Fine.'

'Annie!' hissed the mayor. 'Come back!'

The conversation had ended. Lottie pretended to be engrossed in her book.

The librarian rounded the corner and startled as she saw Lottie there.

'Miss Sprigg!' she said. 'You quite surprised me! Here again?'

'I'm afraid so.'

Walter Campbell appeared behind Miss Roberts and flashed Lottie a jolly grin. 'Didn't I see you at Fortescue Manor the other day?' he said.

'Yes,' said Lottie. 'I work for Lady Buckley-Phipps' sister, Mrs Moore.'

'I thought you looked familiar. I never forget a face!'

'I'm very sorry about your wife,' said Lottie.

'Ah, yes. Thank you. It's been a very difficult time. I'm doing my best to put a brave face on it. I'm visiting the library today to show my support for this wonderful facility we have in the heart of Oswestry. I like to come here every Christmas and thank the staff for all their hard work.'

'That's very thoughtful of you, Mr Campbell.'

'I like to think so, Miss Sprigg. I'd better be on my way. It was nice to see you again, Miss Roberts. Have a lovely Christmas.'

Lottie saw the mayor again as she joined Rosie outside the library. He'd just stepped out of Russell Bank and was whistling a happy tune as he went.

Chapter Twenty-Four

'Psst!' Mildred called out as Lottie and Rosie walked through the saloon on their return to Fortescue Manor. 'We need to speak to Jack,' said Mildred in a loud whisper.

'Jack?'

'Yes, the new footman. You know who I mean, don't you?'

'Yes.' For some reason, Lottie blushed. Maybe it was because she hadn't spoken to him much before. And he was quite handsome, and she'd accidentally caught his eye a few times.

'Are you alright, Lottie?'

'Yes, I'm fine. Does Jack know something?'

'Yes. Come on, let's go and find him.'

As they made their way down the service staircase, Lottie told Mildred about the mayor and the librarian. 'I like to think I'm mistaken,' she added. 'But they seemed quite friendly.'

'You think Mr Campbell is having an affair?'

'I'm sure of it.'

'Poor Mrs Campbell! I wonder if she knew about it?'

· · ·

Jack was standing at a table in the boot room, polishing shoes and boots.

'Oh hello Mildred,' he said. 'And Miss Sprigg.'

'Hello Jack.' He had dark hair which was a little long on top and flopped into his eyes.

'Tell Lottie what you told me,' said Mildred.

'All of it?'

'Yes. She needs to hear it.'

'Where should I start?'

'From when you were dressed up as the elf.'

'Please stop reminding me of that.'

'Go on.'

'Alright.' He turned to Lottie. 'I don't think Mrs Palmer went to the Christmas Fayre,' he said. 'When the mayor came back to the house after opening the Fayre, he got changed into his outfit and said he had a bag of gifts for the servants. He asked me to show him the way to the servants' hall, so I did and Mrs Palmer was there. She was very grateful for the presents and joked she was going to open them all herself while everyone else was at the Fayre.'

'Can you remember what time that was?' asked Lottie.

'About half-past two, I think. Then the mayor told me to go to the drawing room and make sure all the children were forming an orderly queue. He told me he'd join me as soon as he'd visited the bathroom. Five minutes later, he arrived in the drawing room and we began handing out the presents to the children.'

Lottie turned to Mildred. 'Mrs Palmer was here at half-past two. That gave her an hour to get to the grotto.'

'But wait until you hear the next bit,' said Mildred.

'I helped the mayor hand out presents for about an hour,' said Jack.

'I can imagine that was noisy with all those excitable children,' said Lottie.

'It was! I enjoyed it. Although I don't think the mayor did. He seemed quite grumpy and said very little. So I felt I had to act the part of a jolly elf to make up for it.'

'It's a shame he didn't get into the role,' said Lottie. 'I suppose being Father Christmas is a duty not every mayor enjoys.'

'After an hour or so, the mayor wanted a bathroom break,' said Jack. 'So I went down to the servants' hall again to see if there were any spare mince pies going. Mrs Palmer was still there.'

'What was she doing?' asked Lottie.

'She was sitting in a chair, knitting. And she told me how much she was enjoying the peace and quiet.'

'So she couldn't have murdered Mrs Campbell,' said Mildred. 'She was in the servants' hall at the time.'

'And this was at half-past three?' said Lottie.

'I think it was probably a bit later,' said Jack. 'In fact, I think we were handing out the presents until about a quarter to four.'

'So, by the time you'd gone down to the servants' hall, it was probably around ten minutes to four when you saw Mrs Palmer there?'

'Yes, probably.'

'Did you find some mince pies to eat?' asked Lottie.

'Yes.' He smiled. 'I had two. And I was just about to return upstairs when Edward came running in with the news about Mrs Campbell. I had to go and tell the mayor.'

'That can't have been easy.'

'It wasn't. Fortunately, he hadn't yet returned to the drawing room, he'd just come out of the bathroom. And then I had to tell him.' Jack shook his head sadly. 'I don't want to have to do something like that again. Obviously he didn't wish to return to the children in the drawing room, so I had to go in there and explain to everyone there'd been an accident and we had to stop handing out presents.'

'It sounds like you managed it extremely well, Jack,' said Lottie. 'It must have been difficult.'

'It's kind of you to say so, Miss Sprigg. I just did what I could.'

They thanked Jack and left him with the boots and shoes.

'I like Jack,' said Mildred as they walked along the corridor back towards the servants' hall. 'He's nice.'

'He is,' said Lottie. Then she lowered her voice to a whisper. 'But the question is, could Mrs Palmer have got back to the kitchen from the grotto by ten to four?'

'You changed the subject quickly.'

'From what?'

'Jack.' Mildred giggled and nudged Lottie with her elbow.

'Yes, he's nice, and he's been helpful.' She ignored the heat in her face. 'But we need to work out if Mrs Palmer could have got to the grotto and back without being noticed.'

'We could try it ourselves and see how long it takes. Shall we do it this evening?'

'Yes. Good idea!'

Ahead of them in the corridor, someone stepped out of the laundry room.

'Oh hello!'

It was Mrs Palmer. And she looked surprised to see them there.

Chapter Twenty-Five

'I'VE GOT to get back to my dusting,' said Mildred, dashing off and leaving Lottie and Rosie with Mrs Palmer.

Lottie felt uncomfortable being face-to-face with the cook. She felt sure Mrs Palmer would somehow know she suspected her of murder. But she had to make the most of this opportunity to speak to her.

'I'm sorry to hear your husband's gun is missing,' said Lottie. 'He must be very worried about it.'

'Yes, he is. He noticed it was missing after the murder. But we don't know when it was taken. It was kept in a drawer in the sideboard, and he hadn't checked the drawer for a while. So it could have gone missing a while before the attack took place.'

'But can you be sure it was the gun used in the murder?'

'My husband, Ernest, says the gun used in the murder was a Webley revolver. Apparently the police know that from examining the bullets which were fired. His missing gun is a Webley. It's one my nephew brought back from the war. Ernest is worried now the police think he murdered Mrs Campbell.'

87

'Why would he have done that?'

'Because his gun went missing and because... well, I'd kept it quiet, but it seems people have found out. I used to work for Mr and Mrs Campbell. The mayoress dismissed me because she wasn't happy with my cooking. I've never had any complaints from anyone else, so I can only imagine she took a dislike to me. Anyway, Ernest is worried the police will think he shot Mrs Campbell out of revenge.'

'Do you mind me asking what your husband looks like?' asked Lottie.

'What he looks like? Why?'

'I saw Ruth Campbell with a man shortly before her death, and no one knows who he is yet.'

'Well, he wouldn't have been my husband! He's short and wide, with a face like a bulldog. His nickname is Bulldog, actually. Does that sound like the man she was seen with?'

'No,' said Lottie. 'The man was tall, fair and smartly dressed.'

Mrs Palmer laughed. 'My husband has never been smartly dressed in his life! Anyway, I should get on. Let's hope they catch that killer soon.'

Chapter Twenty-Six

LOTTIE TOLD Mrs Moore about her day before dinner that evening.

'I can only hope you're mistaken about Walter Campbell and the librarian,' said Mrs Moore. 'But it sounds likely there's an affair going on. It makes you wonder if he had a hand in his wife's death, doesn't it?'

'It does,' said Lottie. 'It must be quite convenient for him now she's no longer around. But he couldn't have been involved because he was giving out presents to the children at the time. Jack the footman told me all about it. He was the elf.'

'Ah yes, the handsome elf.'

'This evening, Mildred and I are going to see how long it takes to get from the kitchen to the grotto. We want to work out if Mrs Palmer could have got there and back without being noticed by anyone.'

'That would be interesting to find out. I think it would take at least fifteen minutes. But I'm not the fastest moving person. And looking at Mrs Palmer, I can't imagine her being particularly fast moving either. I don't see how she could have got there and back in time. And from Jack's description of her sitting in her chair knitting, she clearly didn't have the appearance of someone who'd just dashed out and murdered someone.'

'True.'

'And besides, what's happening with the mysterious fair-haired man? You'd have thought the detective would have discovered who he was by now. I can't believe nobody knows.'

'When do we need to leave for London?'

'Well, that all depends on when they get the railway line cleared. I wouldn't like to leave any later than the twenty-second. Why do you ask?'

'Because I'd like to visit the orphanage before we leave. I'd like to take Miss Beaufort a gift.'

'And ask about your mother again?'

'Yes.' Lottie sighed. 'There has to be another clue. I've visited the library a lot and I've still not seen her.'

'Perhaps you have, but Miss Beaufort's description wasn't very good.'

'Yes, it's possible. So I'd like to speak to Miss Beaufort again. I had hoped I'd find the lady before Christmas, but I don't think there's any hope of that now.'

Chapter Twenty-Seven

LILY GRANGER SAT in her armchair and viewed her visitor with distaste. What was he doing here? She lit her cigarette, and he lit his pipe.

'I understand you claimed the position of chair at the Lowton Chorley Ladies' Society meeting yesterday evening,' said Detective Inspector Lloyd.

'Who did you hear that from?' It had to have been Annie Roberts. How she hated that woman!

'I've been interviewing a lot of people recently, Mrs Granger, and it was something which I heard during my interviews. As I recall, both you and Mrs Campbell had tied on the number of votes required for the position of chair. I understand there was going to be a new round of voting to determine who would be elected to the position. But at last night's meeting, you claimed the position for yourself.'

'Yes, I thought that would be the most sensible thing to do. Mrs Campbell was no longer in the running because she... well, because she was dead. So I thought the members of the group would naturally accept me as chair.'

'There are some suggestions that you sought to benefit from Mrs Campbell's death by claiming the position of chair.'

'No, not at all, Detective! I would never consider myself as benefiting from someone else's death. How awful! The reasoning behind my suggestion that I become chair was to invite some calm and serenity to the Ladies' Society. We've all been through a tumultuous time, and the vote has divided everybody. I thought it would be extremely harmful to go through yet another round of voting, so that's why I volunteered myself to be chair. After all, half of the people in the group voted for me. So I knew at least half of them would be supportive of me. And I assumed, perhaps wrongly, that the others would also be sympathetic to the situation we found ourselves in. But it wasn't to be.'

'Some people say that you wanted to see off your rival,' said the detective.

'Who's saying such things?' She felt anger building in her chest. 'I don't think it's any secret that Mrs Campbell and I didn't see eye to eye. We both wished to be the chair of the Ladies' Society, and that created some rivalry between us. But if you're suggesting for one moment that I actually murdered her so I could become chair of the Ladies' Society, then that is completely shocking. And I can't believe other people would say such a thing too. It's completely reprehensible!'

'So it's a coincidence that you found Mrs Campbell in the grotto?'

'Nothing more than a coincidence, Detective.'

'Because it's possible you could have followed her up to the grotto with a gun in your handbag, then committed the deed when she was alone up there.'

'I had no idea she was there!'

'You say that, Mrs Granger, but there's still a possibility, isn't there? Can you see the dilemma I'm posed with? You found Mrs Campbell in the grotto, deceased. And I only have your word for it you're not responsible. We also know there was rivalry between the pair of you. Only a day after Mrs Campbell's death, you proclaimed yourself chair of the Ladies' Society. It's rather convenient for you that Mrs Campbell is out of the way, isn't it?'

'Oh, stop it, Detective! It simply isn't true!'

Chapter Twenty-Eight

LOTTIE AND ROSIE met Mildred in the corridor outside the servants' hall. They were wrapped up in warm clothes and Lottie had put a woollen dog coat on Rosie.

'I've just checked the kitchen,' whispered Mildred, as she gave Lottie a torch. 'There's no one in there at the moment, so let's go now.'

Once they were in the kitchen, Lottie checked her watch. 'It's exactly eight o'clock,' she said. 'Let's see how long this takes.'

They climbed the steps from the kitchen to the servants' courtyard and turned right into the grounds of the house. Then they headed for the rose garden, following the path to the grotto.

It was snowing again and thick snowflakes were illuminated by their torch beams. Rosie trotted on ahead, clearly excited to be out on an evening adventure.

'If Mrs Palmer came this way, she would've had to walk carefully to avoid slipping,' said Lottie. 'In fact, I don't see how anyone could run in this.'

They passed the rose garden, which was little more than a

94

few sorry-looking stalks at this time of year. It was difficult to imagine it filled with sweet-scented blooms in the summer months.

The hoot of an owl carried through the night air, and Lottie shivered.

'That sounds creepy!' said Mildred. 'I like owls, and I know it's nothing to be afraid of. But it's spooky when you're out at night, isn't it?'

The path sloped down to the grotto, and they had to tread carefully in the snow.

Eventually they reached the entrance and Lottie shone her torch on her watch. 'It's almost a quarter past eight. I don't think Mrs Palmer could have walked much faster than we did just then, could she?'

'No, I don't think so,' said Mildred. 'The detective says the murder was committed at half-past three and Jack saw Mrs Palmer at ten minutes to four, looking cosy in her chair in the servants' hall and knitting. She could have just about managed it.'

'But I think it would take slightly longer on the way back because you have to walk uphill,' said Lottie. 'And Mrs Palmer would have had to have worn an overcoat and boots in this weather. So, if she's the murderer, she somehow got back to the house and changed out of her outdoor clothes and made herself comfortable in the servants' hall within the space of twenty minutes.'

'It doesn't seem likely, does it?' said Mildred.

'No.'

'Shall we go inside?' said Mildred.

'I suppose so. Although this place gives me the creeps.'

They stepped into the grotto and their torch beams picked out the thousands of little decorative shells on the grotto walls. Lottie shuddered and tried not to think about what had happened there.

'The police must have searched this place for the gun,' said Mildred. 'I wonder if they checked the little passageway at the back?'

'They must have,' said Lottie.

'But it wouldn't hurt to check, would it?'

'No.' Lottie noticed Rosie remained by the grotto entrance, just as she had on their visit here during the summer.

Mildred walked to the back of the grotto and to the passageway at the back. Lottie reluctantly followed.

It was a narrow passageway with walls covered in shells like the rest of the grotto. 'I've never understood the purpose of this passageway,' said Lottie. 'It's just a dead end.'

'Maybe there was a plan to make it longer?'

'Maybe there was. Perhaps there were plans to add something at the end, like a small altar. It's strange that it just stops.'

They stood at the end of the passageway, shining their torches at the walls and floor.

Then something caught Lottie's eye.

She stepped closer to the end wall and crouched down. As she shone her torch at the base of the wall, she could see a gap. It was only small, no bigger than an eighth of an inch. But it ran along the width of the wall.

Then she ran her torch beam up either side of the wall.

'Look at this, Mildred. There's a small gap all around here. If you look at the other walls in this grotto, the shells decorate every surface with no gaps at all. But here, there are gaps.'

'What do you mean?'

'Come closer and you'll be able to see.'

Mildred did so. 'That's strange,' she said.

'Do you know what I think?' said Lottie. 'I think this could be a door.'

Chapter Twenty-Nine

'A DOOR,' said Mildred. 'Leading to where?'

Lottie stepped up to the wall, rested her shoulder against it, and gave it a cautious shove. It gave way slightly. 'It is a door! And it's moving!'

'But what's behind it?' said Mildred. 'A tomb?'

'I hope not.' Lottie shivered. 'But we have to see what's behind the door, don't we?' She pushed against the heavy door and it swung open.

They were met with cold air and darkness.

'Oh, I don't like it!' said Mildred.

Lottie shone her torch into the dark and saw a set of steps leading upwards. 'This must be a secret passage!'

'To where?'

'To the house?'

'But how come I've never heard about this secret passage before?'

'I don't know. I've not heard about it either. We shall have to see where it leads.'

'Alright then.'

'I'll fetch Rosie.' Lottie went back to the grotto entrance

and tried to encourage her reluctant dog to join them. 'Come on, Rosie. Come with us. We found a secret passageway!'

Rosie didn't move.

'There's no need to be scared,' said Lottie. But as she said the words, she felt a tightening in her stomach. She didn't want to walk through a cold, dark tunnel beneath the grounds of Fortescue Manor. But they couldn't possibly leave without discovering where it led.

'I'm going to have to carry you, aren't I?' She walked over to the corgi, picked her up, and carried her back to the passage. Rosie licked her face.

'Won't she walk?' asked Mildred.

'I don't think so, but let's see.' Lottie placed Rosie on the ground in the dark passageway and the little dog stood close by her. Then she walked forward and encouraged Rosie to follow.

The dog remained where she was.

'It's no use,' said Lottie. 'I'm going to have to carry her.' She picked up Rosie again. With the dog in her arms, she had little freedom in her hand to direct her torch beam. 'You'll have to lead the way, Mildred.'

'Me?'

'Rosie and I are right behind you.'

'Okay.'

Mildred stepped forward, and all three made their way into the tunnel. The ceiling was low, only a few inches above Lottie's head. She imagined someone like Barty would have to stoop to make their way through here.

'How many steps are there?' Mildred shone her torch ahead and they could see the flight of steps curving to the right. 'Oh, this is creepy!'

'But we've got to do it, haven't we?' said Lottie. She felt a prickle on the back of her neck.

'Yes, we have.'

The air in the tunnel felt colder than the air outside. And it smelt of musty damp.

They walked cautiously up the old stone steps. 'These look as old as the grotto,' said Lottie. 'I think it was built about two hundred years ago.'

She didn't like the way her voice echoed in the tunnel. It sounded like another person was speaking, too.

They rounded the bend, and the steps levelled out into a corridor that bent to the left. The floor was paved and there were large patches of damp on the walls. Lottie could hear a dripping noise from somewhere.

'I'd hoped it would be a short passageway,' said Mildred. 'But it looks quite long!'

They continued on their way. The tunnel was leading them uphill, and they encountered a few more sets of steps.

'This looks like the sort of place which could be haunted,' said Mildred.

'Oh, don't say that!'

'Do you think Hector the Hermit walked here?'

'I don't know.'

'Perhaps his ghost still walks here?' Mildred stopped. 'Oh, I don't want to carry on! I'm worried I might turn the corner and he'll be standing there!'

A cold shiver ran down Lottie's spine. 'He won't be,' she said, desperately hoping to believe it. 'There's no such thing as ghosts.'

She was trying to convince herself rather than Mildred. She didn't believe in ghosts in the middle of the day. But a dark tunnel at night was making her question it. 'Let's walk on,' she said, her heart thudding. 'Hopefully we can get out of here very soon.'

The air was oppressive. Rosie was getting heavy in Lottie's arms and she felt desperate now to reach the end of the tunnel.

They rounded a bend and found themselves at the bottom of a steep flight of steps. At the top was a wooden door.

'The end!' said Mildred, skipping up the steps. Then she paused. 'It had better not be a tomb!'

'I'm sure it won't be,' said Lottie. 'Can you open the door?'

The door had a handle and a lock on it. Mildred slowly turned the handle and pushed the door, then she gave it a little pull. 'No. I think it must be locked.'

Lottie sighed. They had braved the dark tunnel to find themselves at a locked door. She placed Rosie on the ground and shone her torch on her watch. 'It's twenty-five minutes past eight,' she said. 'If this door is in the basement of the house, then I estimate we've got here in little more than five minutes.'

'But how do we know we're in the basement of the house?' asked Mildred.

'We can't be sure, can we? But the passageway leads uphill, and you have to walk uphill to get to the house from the grotto.'

'So what do we do now? Should we knock on the door and see if someone opens it from the other side?'

'Alright then, let's try it.'

Mildred rapped on the door, and the noise echoed loudly in the tunnel. They waited for a response, but none came.

Mildred tried again. But there was still no answer.

'If this door connects with the house, then it must be in a place where people don't pass by very often,' said Lottie. 'All we can do now is go back to the grotto and walk to the house through the garden.'

'Go back through the tunnel again?'

'It's all we can do.'

'Oh no!'

'But it won't take long. Then we can get back to the house and find out who knows about this passageway. I highly suspect the murderer knew it was here.'

Chapter Thirty

BACK AT THE HOUSE, Lottie and Rosie went to the drawing room where Lord and Lady Buckley-Phipps, Barty and Mrs Moore were playing cards.

'I'm so sorry to interrupt, my lord and lady,' she said. 'But I've found a secret tunnel.'

Everyone stared at her.

'A secret tunnel?' said Lord Buckley-Phipps. 'Where?'

'From the grotto. Mildred and I visited the grotto this evening.'

'On a cold and snowy night? Why?'

Lottie didn't want to admit they suspected the cook and had been trying to work out how long it took to get there from the kitchen. 'We noticed it was snowing outside and wanted to go for an evening walk in it,' she said. 'We found ourselves by the grotto and decided to look inside. Just in case there were any clues in there the police had missed. We discovered a door at the end of the passageway at the back of the grotto.'

'A door?' said Lord Buckley-Phipps. 'I don't believe there's a door there.'

'When did you last visit the grotto, Ivan?' asked his wife.

'I can't say it's a place I visit that often. I poked my head in there to look at the pretty lights during the Christmas Fayre, but I don't think I've been down that passageway for many years. I went maybe once or twice when I was a boy. But I found it a rather scary experience back then and didn't hang around there too long.'

'I should think the same could be said for most people who visit that place,' said Lady Buckley-Phipps. 'I think I've only been in that passageway once, and I didn't stay for long either.'

'So, there's a door at the end of the passageway?' asked Barty.

Lottie nodded.

'And you went through it?'

'Yes. We were able to push the door open, and it led into a tunnel. It had a lot of steps and led uphill. I'm fairly certain it led to the house. But we found a door at the end of it which was locked.'

'And you think that locked door could be in this house?' said Lady Buckley-Phipps.

'I can't be certain,' said Lottie. 'But I think it must be. I only wish we could have got through the door to find out.'

'There's only one thing for it,' said Lord Buckley-Phipps. He rang the bell for the butler.

'You rang, my lord?' asked Mr Duxbury as he arrived in the room.

'Ever heard of a secret tunnel between the house and the grotto, Duxbury?'

'No, my lord.'

'Can you fetch me the house plans, please, Duxbury? I would like to examine them.'

'Of course, my lord. I believe they're in the attic, so it may take me a while to find them.'

'Of course. Just do your best, Duxbury.'

'A secret tunnel,' said Barty. 'Well, I never. Why don't we know about it?'

'I don't know, Barty,' said Lord Buckley-Phipps. 'I've spent my entire life in this house and never knew a thing about the secret tunnel. As a boy, I wished there was a secret door, passageway or tunnel of some sort, but I never found one. I was a little disappointed about that. After all, every large house should have a secret passageway, shouldn't it?'

'And now you have your wish, Ivan,' said Lady Buckley-Phipps.

'I don't think Mother or Father could have known about it, either. Otherwise, they would have mentioned it.'

'So this poses an interesting question,' said Mrs Moore. 'Did Mrs Campbell's murderer know about the secret passage-way? Did they use it to get to the grotto?'

'I don't see how they could have known about it if the rest of us didn't,' said Lord Buckley-Phipps.

'But it could explain how the killer got to and from the crime without being noticed by anybody else.'

'Ah, but what about the fair-haired man seen with Mrs Campbell?' said Lord Buckley-Phipps. 'He's surely the main suspect. If the killer used the tunnel to get to the grotto, then that means he or she must be a member of this household. And I refuse to believe anyone here could have committed such a crime!'

'What about Mr Palmer's gun?' said Lady Buckley-Phipps. 'It was used in the murder, wasn't it? That suggests the killer could be someone from the household. Or a worker on the estate.'

'But that could have been taken by anyone, Lucinda.'

'I won't hear accusations against members of our house-hold! It's that mysterious fair-haired man who's responsible and Detective Inspector Lloyd needs to arrest him as soon as possible.'

'I don't think we can ignore the possibility the killer could have used that tunnel,' said Mrs Moore.

'But who could possibly have known about it if neither I nor Lucinda knew?' said Lord Buckley-Phipps. 'And Barty didn't know about it, did you, Barty?'

The young man shook his head. 'No. Nor did I ever hear anyone talking about it.'

'And Mr Duxbury didn't know about it,' said Lady Buckley-Phipps.

'Maybe someone discovered it by accident?' said Barty.

'And then somehow used that knowledge to commit a terrible murder?' said Lord Buckley-Phipps. He shook his head. 'No, I don't think I can quite believe that.'

A short while later, Mr Duxbury returned to the room with a large roll of paper under one arm.

'Ah ha!' said Lord Buckley-Phipps. 'The house plans!'

'Indeed, my lord.' The butler used his spare hand to brush dust from his sleeves and jacket.

'Spread them out on the table over there, Duxbury, and let's get a good look at them. We need to find the door which Lottie described at the end of the tunnel.'

Mr Duxbury did so, then everyone gathered around the table. The rolled-up ends of the plans were weighed down by ash trays and ornaments the butler had purloined from various parts of the room.

'How interesting,' said Lord Buckley-Phipps. 'Fortescue Manor is bigger than I realised.'

Lottie peered at the carefully drawn plans. There was a sheet for each floor of the house, including the basement and the attics.

'It's fascinating to see the house drawn in this way,' said Mrs Moore.

Lottie spotted a date. 'It looks like these were drawn up in 1882,' she said.

'That makes sense,' said Lord Buckley-Phipps. 'I believe some alterations were made around that time by my grandfather. He would have commissioned these plans.'

'I can't see a secret tunnel on here, though,' said Mrs Moore.

'Neither can I,' said Lady Buckley-Phipps.

'It has to lead to a door in the basement,' said Lottie.

They examined the basement.

'There's the kitchen,' said Lord Buckley-Phipps, pressing a chubby forefinger on it. 'And there's the servants' hall. Over here we have the butler's and housekeeper's rooms. I can also see the laundry room, gun room, boiler room, boot room and... so many rooms! And lots of storage cupboards, too.'

From her knowledge of the house during the time she'd worked there as a maid, Lottie could identify most of the rooms in the basement. As she looked closer, what appeared to be a storage room in the laundry caught her eye.

'What's this room here?' she said. 'It seems to have a door leading to nowhere.'

Everybody peered closer.

'So it does!' said Lord Buckley-Phipps.

'Perhaps Miss Hudson will know about it,' said Mr Duxbury. He went to fetch the housekeeper and returned with her a moment later.

'It's a storage room within the laundry room,' said Miss Hudson. 'We don't really use it for anything. From memory, I think there are some old washtubs kept there.'

'And the door?'

'I don't think there's a door in there.'

'There's a door marked on this plan.'

'Perhaps it's a mistake?'

'Well, there's only one thing for it,' said Lord Buckley-Phipps. 'We have to go down there and have a look!'

Chapter Thirty-One

'Isn't this exciting, Lottie?' said Mrs Moore as they made their way out of the drawing room and headed to the service stairs, which led to the basement. 'You've caused some entertainment for us this evening!'

Everyone followed Miss Hudson through the stone corridors which linked the kitchen and servants' hall. They passed the boot room, the gun room and several storerooms until they reached the laundry room.

Miss Hudson switched on the light to reveal a low-ceilinged room with a tiled floor. There was a row of sinks along one wall and traditional mangles stood next to a new electric washing machine. It was shaped like a half barrel and stood on four metal legs. Household linen and garments hung on a large drying rack suspended from the ceiling. Lottie liked the clean, soapy smell of the room.

'From the plan, I think that storeroom with the door is this one here,' said the housekeeper. She opened the door. 'Old wash tubs,' she said. Four of them stacked in a tower. 'We put them in here when we got the electric machine,' she said.

'But where's the door?' asked Lord Buckley-Phipps.

'I'll move these wash tubs out, my lord. Then we can get a better look.'

'I'll do it, Miss Hudson.' Mr Duxbury picked up the stack of tubs and placed it by the sinks. Then he examined the floor. 'Interesting,' he said. 'There looks to be a trapdoor in this floor.'

'Open it, Duxbury!' said Lord Buckley-Philips.

'Very well, my lord.'

Everyone was quiet as the butler bent down, put his finger under the loop on the hatch, and pulled it up.

'That opened quite easily,' he said.

'What's down there?' asked Lady Buckley-Phipps.

'It's too dark to see, my lady. Has anybody got a torch?'

'I have,' said Lottie, handing him the torch she had used earlier in the grotto.

The butler took it from her and shone it into the hatch. 'There's a small ladder here, my lord. And I do believe I can see a door.'

'Wonderful!' said Lord Buckley-Phipps. 'Can you get down there and try the door, Duxbury?'

'I will do, my lord.'

They waited as he carefully descended the ladder and stood in the little compartment beneath the floor. 'I can see a full-sized door in front of me here, my lord,' he called up.

'And does it open?' asked Lord Buckley-Phipps.

'No, my lord. It's locked shut.'

'Miss Hudson,' said Lord Buckley-Phipps. 'Could you please pass your bunch of keys to Mr Duxbury, and he can try each of them in the lock.'

'Yes, my lord.' She unclipped the bunch of keys from her belt and handed it down to the butler. 'But I can account for every one of these keys and which doors they open. I don't think we'll find the key for the door down there. I shall have a look in my office, there are more keys there which I use less frequently. Perhaps one of those might fit.'

'Thank you, Miss Hudson. I suppose we can't be certain yet that this door leads to the secret tunnel.'

'I think it must do, Ivan,' said his wife. 'After all, the laundry room is at the rear of the house in the basement. If you think about it, it's really not too far to the grotto from here if there's a tunnel directly under the ground.'

Lord Buckley-Phipps called down the hatch to the butler. 'Have you had any luck down there with the keys, Duxbury?'

'Not yet, my lord,' came the reply.

Miss Hudson returned with more keys.

'Excellent,' said Lord Buckley-Phipps. 'Can you pass them down to Duxbury please, Miss Hudson? Surely one of those must fit the lock.'

'If we're having this much trouble finding a key that fits the lock,' said Lady Buckley-Phipps. 'Then how on earth did the killer find the key?'

'We don't know for sure if the killer used this route, Lucinda,' said her husband. 'Let's not get ahead of ourselves.'

Rosie grew bored and wandered around the laundry room sniffing at things. After a while, Mr Duxbury had tried every key that could be recovered from across the house, and not one of them opened the door.

'That's a shame,' said Lord Buckley-Phipps. 'Can you break it down?'

'I'd rather call the locksmith tomorrow morning, my lord.'

'Ah yes, that's a more sensible idea. We shall have to wait until tomorrow then. How disappointing.'

Chapter Thirty-Two

LILY GRANGER STROLLED down Lowton Chorley High Street with her shopping basket looped over her arm. It was a bright, sunny morning, and she was looking forward to getting her Christmas shopping finished. She was wrapped up warm in her fur-trimmed coat and she acknowledged every familiar face with a red-lipsticked smile.

She paused at the toy shop window, looking for something suitable for her nieces and nephews. Snow globes, teddy bears, colourful toy soldiers and a rocking horse were arranged around a Christmas tree adorned with colourful ribbons and baubles. Some little children ran up to the window, pointing and chattering excitedly. Lily couldn't bear their noise, so she moved on to the bakery shop.

She was admiring an enormous gingerbread house expertly decorated with icing and sweets when someone joined her at the window. 'Goodness, what an impressive gingerbread house. I wonder how long it took the baker to make that.'

Lily turned to see blonde-haired Annie Roberts next to her. 'Oh, it's you.'

'Hello Lily. Doing some Christmas shopping?'

'Yes. Aren't you needed in the library?'

'I've closed it for ten minutes just so I could pop out and do a few things.'

'That's no way to provide a public service.'

'It's been quiet this morning.'

'There could be someone waiting outside it at this very moment.'

'I won't be long.'

'Good.' Now was Lily's opportunity to confront her about the role of chair of the Lowton Chorley Ladies' Society. 'You're making a big mistake going for chair, you know. No one's going to vote for you.'

'You're only saying that because you don't want any competition.'

Lily laughed. 'What nonsense! I'm happy to have competition because I know I'll win.'

'But you didn't win the last vote, did you?'

'I almost did. And I can see now why you wanted to block my accession to the role of chair. It's purely because you want it for yourself. All your talk about doing what's best for the Ladies' Society is nonsense. You only have your own interests at heart.'

'I asked everyone present if they agreed with me, and they did. It's only fair that another vote is held.'

Lily had to frighten her off the idea. She'd waited years to become the chair, and she wasn't about to let the silly little librarian stop her.

'I could make life very difficult for you, you know.'

'And how do you intend to do that?'

'I've seen you with *him*.'

'I don't know what you mean.'

'You know exactly what I mean. Wouldn't it be awful if people found out about it?'

'If you think you can blackmail me, then you're wrong!'

'It's not blackmail, Annie. All I need to do is simply tell people the truth. And anyway, don't flatter yourself that you're anyone special. He tried to charm me a few months ago, and I batted him away.'

'You're lying!'

'I wish I was. I also have another piece of advice for you.'

'Advice? Or another threat?'

'Stop talking to the police about me.'

'The police? I haven't spoken to them.'

'So how does Detective Inspector Lloyd know about our meeting the other evening?'

'I don't know. I can only guess one of the attendees was suspicious about you claiming the role of chair the day after Mrs Campbell's death.'

'If I find out it was you who spoke to the detective, I really will cause trouble for you. And that boyfriend of yours. I know a few things about him too.'

'Such as what?'

'You don't want to find out, believe me. Anyway, I'd better get on. If I were you, I'd have a long, hard think about whether putting yourself forward for the chair is a good idea.'

Chapter Thirty-Three

AFTER BREAKFAST AT FORTESCUE MANOR, word spread that the locksmith had opened the door in the laundry storage room.

'His lordship is giving us a half-hour break so we can all go and investigate the tunnel!' said Mildred. 'Now we can find out if it's the same tunnel we walked along.'

'It must be,' said Lottie. 'Surely there can't be two secret tunnels?' She and Rosie followed Mildred to the laundry room where everyone was gathering. Mrs Moore and Barty chatted excitedly, and Mr Duxbury held a large paraffin lamp.

Lord and Lady Buckley-Phipps joined them.

'Is everyone here?' asked Lord Buckley-Phipps.

'Mrs Palmer isn't, my lord,' said Jack.

'Why not? Does she know what she's missing out on?'

'She says she doesn't like dark, enclosed spaces, my lord.'

Lottie and Mildred exchanged a glance. Was it a genuine reason? Or was it because she was the murderer and didn't wish to return to the scene of the crime?

'Very well,' said Lord Buckley-Phipps. 'Now, the ladder

which leads down to the door is quite sturdy, but some of you ladies may be a little alarmed using it. Don't fear. It's only about six feet long. Duxbury will descend the ladder first and assist the ladies. We gentlemen will bring up the rear. Once we're all down there, Duxbury will light the way with his lamp and I shall walk with him. The rest of you can follow. Barty, please bring up the rear and make sure we don't leave anyone behind. Onwards!'

Lord Buckley-Phipps was clearly enjoying the adventure.

Lottie passed Rosie down to Mrs Moore once her employer had descended the ladder. Then she climbed down and waited for the others to descend.

It took a while and eventually everyone was squeezed into the small space by the door.

'Mind the steps on the other side of the door,' said Lord Buckley-Phipps, pushing his way through to the front. 'Light the way, Duxbury!'

Once again, Rosie was reluctant to walk into the tunnel, so Lottie carried her.

'Isn't it dark?' said Lady Buckley-Phipps.

'Of course it's dark, Mother,' said Barty. 'We're going underground!' They climbed down the steps and made their way through the tunnel. It looked familiar to Lottie and felt much less scary now it was filled with people.

'I wonder why this tunnel was built,' said Lord Buckley-Phipps. 'Why would anyone have wanted to build a secret route to the grotto?'

'Maybe the Lord Buckley-Phipps who built it used it for secret assignations,' called out Barty from the back.

'What? Are you suggesting one of our ancestors had dalliances?'

'I thought they all did in those days, Father.'

'Not the Buckley-Phipps family. We've always upheld our standards.'

They continued on their way, descending more steps as they went.

Suddenly they were plunged into darkness.

Lady Buckley-Phipps let out a cry.

'Duxbury? What's happened?' said her husband.

'The lamp has gone out, my lord.'

'Can't you relight it?'

'I'm trying to, my lord. But it doesn't seem to be working. There's a rather cold draught down here which keeps extinguishing the flame.'

'Perhaps you can turn on your torch instead.'

'I didn't bring my torch with me, my lord. I thought this lamp would suffice. It's a very good lamp. I've never known it to do this before.'

'Can someone else please switch on their torch?' said Lord Buckley-Phipps.

After some muttering, it appeared nobody had brought a torch with them.

'Are you telling me that the only light source we brought down here was one paltry paraffin lamp?' said Lord Buckley-Phipps.

'Oh, good heavens!' said his wife. 'I hate the dark! I can't even see my own hand in front of my face. It's just awful. I feel like I've been buried alive!'

'Calm down, Mother,' said Barty. 'You haven't been buried alive at all. We're all here with you. I'm sure Duxbury will get that lamp lit in a moment, and then all will be fine again.'

They waited as the butler tried to light the lamp. It sparked but didn't produce a flame.

'Oh, this is very unfortunate indeed,' lamented Lady Buckley-Phipps. 'It's not going to light, is it? What are we going to do now?'

'Well, we'll have to continue in the dark,' said her husband.

'Without a light?'

'Well, what else do you suggest, Lucinda? Hopefully, this leads to the grotto. Once we're there, we can get outside and return to the house through the garden.'

'But I didn't bring the right shoes for walking through the snow! I only brought shoes appropriate for walking through the tunnel. These aren't waterproof at all!'

'Well, I'm afraid that when you're going on an adventure, Lucinda, you must prepare for all eventualities. Would you rather wait here in the dark while Duxbury goes off to fetch a light?'

'No, I don't want to stay here! But I also don't know how we're going to find our way through the tunnel in the dark. It has lots of steps and is quite uneven underfoot. In fact, I don't see how we're going to get out of here at all!'

'Well, standing around talking won't help us, Lucinda,' said Mrs Moore. 'All we can do is continue in the dark.'

'Sounds like a good plan to me,' said Barty.

Lottie wasn't fond of the darkness, either. But Rosie seemed unbothered. As a dog, her eyesight was much better accustomed to the gloom.

Progress towards the grotto slowed significantly. Mr Duxbury advanced for a few yards, then called them all forward with instructions about steps and the uneven floor. It was a painstakingly slow process, and the initial excitement of following the secret tunnel had faded. The mood was subdued until they reached the door at the end.

'I can feel a door in front of me,' Mr Duxbury said. 'I pushed against it, but it won't budge.'

'You need to pull it,' said Lottie. 'Can you find a handle?'

After some searching, the butler pulled the door open, and the tunnel was flooded with dim grey light.

'It's the grotto!' announced Lord Buckley-Phipps.

They made their way into the passageway, and Lottie felt the uneven, decorative stones beneath her feet. As they stepped into the main part of the grotto, the sunshine from outside was dazzling. Lottie placed Rosie on the ground and she scampered over to the entrance.

'Well, here we are,' said Mrs Moore. 'We finally made it to the grotto!'

'Is everyone alright walking to the house through the snow?' said Lord Buckley-Phipps. 'Or shall I ask Duxbury to fetch a torch from the house and take us back through the tunnel?'

'I'll walk through the snow,' said his wife. 'It will ruin my shoes, but I'm not setting foot in that miserable tunnel again.'

Chapter Thirty-Four

THERE WAS NO ONE ABOUT. They'd all gone down the creepy tunnel.

Hannah Palmer retrieved the bag from a cupboard in the servants' hall and stepped out into the corridor.

She made her way past the service stairs, the trunk room, and the door leading to the housekeeper's rooms. Then she turned right and passed another staircase, the sewing room, the laundry room, and the gun room.

She stopped and turned the gun room door handle. It was still locked.

Hannah went on her way and continued to the small door at the end of the corridor. She took out a key and unlocked it.

Then she opened the door.

'Hello!' she said. 'I'm a little earlier than usual today.'

Chapter Thirty-Five

AT THE HOUSE, Detective Inspector Lloyd was waiting for them in the entrance hall, puffing on his pipe.

'I apologise for keeping you waiting, Detective,' said Lord Buckley-Phipps. 'But we've just discovered a secret tunnel which leads from the house to the grotto.'

The detective raised an eyebrow. 'A secret tunnel, my lord? You've just discovered it?'

'Yes! It's probably been there for over two hundred years and no one knew! Come on through to the sitting room. Lady Buckley-Phipps will join us once she's changed her shoes.'

'Very well. It's the young ladies I need to speak to.'

'Which ones?'

'Miss Sprigg and Miss Mallet.'

Mildred gave Lottie a concerned glance as they followed the detective and Lord Buckley-Phipps to the sitting room.

'Here are the house plans,' said Lord Buckley-Phipps. He showed the detective where the tunnel led from.

'This is very interesting indeed, my lord. This widens my investigation, as it suggests that the killer could have used the tunnel to commit the attack or make a quick getaway.'

'I don't believe the killer could be someone from this house,' said Lord Buckley-Phipps.

'I understand your concern, my lord. It could have been someone who was aware of the secret tunnel and sneaked into the house's basement to access it.'

'It's a possibility. Although I don't find that idea appealing either.'

'But if the murderer did use that route, we may find some clues in the tunnel.'

'You might, Detective, although we didn't discover any clues during our exploration of it just now.'

The detective frowned. 'You've visited the tunnel?'

'Yes. Miss Sprigg and Miss Mallet discovered it last night and we've all explored it just now. We couldn't find a key, so we had to get a locksmith to open the door for us.'

'How many people explored it?'

'Oh, I don't know. Nine, ten, maybe? Possibly more.'

The detective sighed. 'So any clues left by the murderer will have been disturbed.'

'I don't believe there were any clues, Detective.' Lord Buckley-Phipps turned to Lottie and Mildred. 'Did you see any clues when you walked through the tunnel last night?'

Lottie shook her head. 'No, my lord.'

'There you go, Detective, no clues were discovered.'

'Clues can be subtle, my lord. For instance, a few threads snagged from the murderer's coat. Such evidence might have been brushed away by the people in the tunnel. With so many people wandering about down there, potential evidence may have been compromised.'

'I think you're making a bit of a fuss, Lloyd. The only way to discover where that tunnel led was to go down it! And besides, the murderer is clearly the man who was seen with Mrs Campbell shortly before her death. He wouldn't have had any idea the tunnel was there.'

'Talking of which, I need to speak to these two young ladies,' said Detective Inspector Lloyd. He pulled out a photograph from a pocket inside his jacket and held it up.

'Can I ask if you recognise this man?' The photograph showed a smartly dressed, fair-haired gentleman.

Lottie recognised him immediately. 'Yes! He was the gentleman I saw with Mrs Campbell as she was walking to the grotto.'

The detective turned to Mildred. 'And what do you think, Miss Mallet?'

Mildred nodded. 'Lottie's right. He looks just like the man we saw.'

'Thank you very much.' The detective put the photograph back in his jacket pocket.

'Well?' said Lord Buckley-Phipps. 'Who is he?'

'He's a solicitor and his name is Peter Harris.'

'So he's a solicitor for the Campbell family?'

'Not the family, as such. He told me he was being retained by Mrs Campbell for a personal matter.'

'I'm surprised Walter Campbell didn't recognise the description of him.'

'That's probably because Mr Campbell isn't particularly familiar with him. The solicitor is a relative newcomer to Lowton Chorley. He was helping Mrs Campbell with a private matter. A matter considered so sensitive that he approached me quietly and with no fanfare at all to explain what happened that afternoon. It wouldn't be fair to the Campbell family to publicise the nature of his business with Mrs Campbell.'

Mildred's mouth dropped open. 'They were having an affair?'

'Absolutely not!' said the detective. 'Mr Harris assures me their relationship was purely professional. They hadn't planned to meet at the Fayre, but they'd bumped into each other and Mrs Campbell requested an urgent word. The pair walked together to the grotto, and that's when you saw them. Apparently Mrs Campbell had arranged to meet a friend at the grotto at half-past three.'

'Which friend?' said Lord Buckley-Phipps.

'Mr Harris didn't know.'

'I think it's quite apparent that friend must be the murderer!'

'Possibly.'

'Possibly? It's obvious!'

'I shall conduct some further investigations, my lord.'

Lottie wondered if Mrs Campbell had been consulting her solicitor about a divorce. Was it possible she'd discovered the affair between Mr Campbell and Miss Roberts?

'I'm sure I can trust you young ladies to keep this information to yourself,' said the detective. 'I've little doubt that eventually word will get out that Mrs Campbell was consulting a solicitor. But it's only fair to Mr Campbell that this information isn't widely talked about. It certainly puts an end to the mystery which had been troubling me from the outset. Establishing the identity of the mystery gentleman wasn't easy. But I can understand why he was reluctant to shout about it, and I feel reassured he had nothing to do with the crime.'

'It sounds like you need to find the mysterious friend now, Detective,' said Lord Buckley-Phipps. 'Any word yet on help from Scotland Yard?'

'Last night's snowfall has hindered any progress in clearing the railway line between London and Shrewsbury, my lord. Our colleague from the Yard is still unable to reach us.'

'Can't we provide him with a car?'

'As I understand it, my lord, the roads on this side of the country are rather treacherous. I'll certainly inquire with the

Yard to see if that's a possibility, but we're making good progress as it is.'

'Are we?'

'Yes.' He blew out a puff of pipe smoke. 'Now perhaps you could show me this secret tunnel, my lord?'

Chapter Thirty-Six

LOTTIE TOLD Mrs Moore about the conversation with Detective Inspector Lloyd as they took a little walk in the snowy gardens before lunch.

'I wonder how the detective can be so sure that the solicitor didn't harm Mrs Campbell,' said Lottie.

'Probably because he's a solicitor,' said Mrs Moore. 'It's less common for respectable gentlemen to commit such horrible crimes. But it's not unheard of, is it?'

'No, it's not. If I were investigating the case, then he would be a suspect. But maybe the detective knows some information which we don't.'

'Perhaps. And it seems that Mrs Campbell had arranged to meet a friend at the grotto. Surely that friend must be the murderer?'

'But we only have Mr Harris's word for it,' said Lottie. 'Perhaps he is the murderer, and the supposed arrangement to meet a friend is a lie.'

'Golly! That's a good point, Lottie. He could easily be saying such a thing to cover his tracks, couldn't he?'

Rosie chased after a pigeon which had been pecking about in the snow. It flew lazily away.

'Poor pigeon,' said Lottie. 'It must struggle to find food with all this snow on the ground.'

'But no one's allowed to put out any food for them,' said Mrs Moore. 'Lord Buckley-Phipps keeps complaining about the vermin. Anyway, back to Mr Harris, the solicitor. If he is the murderer, then I suppose we can forget all about the secret tunnel from the house, can't we? He wouldn't have even gone into the house. There would have been no need for him to use the secret tunnel.'

'There's still the cook, Mrs Palmer, to consider,' said Lottie. 'Mildred and I went to the grotto last night to work out if she could have got there and back in time before she was seen by Jack in the servants' hall at ten to four. When we first got to the grotto, we discovered the route would have taken too long. But then we discovered the secret tunnel.'

'Which shortens it! So she could have got there and back?'

'Yes, I think so.'

'She didn't join us in the tunnel, did she? Perhaps she couldn't bring herself to return to the grotto. We also know she had a motive for harming Mrs Campbell and her husband's gun is missing! Perhaps she's the person who arranged to meet Mrs Campbell?'

Chapter Thirty-Seven

'THERE'S no easy way of putting this, Mr Campbell,' said Detective Inspector Lloyd. They sat in Walter's sitting room. Walter was wearing his mayoral chain over his pullover to remind the detective of his status.

'Just hit me with it,' he said. 'After everything I've been through these past few days, I'm sure it's nothing I can't stomach.'

'We've identified the gentleman who your wife was walking with to the grotto shortly before her death.'

'Who is he? Have you arrested him?'

'There's no need to arrest him, Mr Campbell. I'm sure he had nothing to do with your wife's death.'

'She was being escorted by an unknown gentleman to the grotto shortly before she was murdered, and yet you don't suspect him? What do you mean by this, Detective?'

'He has proven to be a very reliable witness.'

'Reliable is he? How do you know he's not lying to you?'

'I'm quite certain he isn't.'

'I don't see what makes you so sure.'

'There are reasons which I shall go into shortly, Mr Campbell.'

'So what was it, then? An affair?'

'No, it wasn't.' Although Mr Campbell felt reassured by this, he was also puzzled.

'So you need to tell me who he was.'

'His name is Mr Harris, and he's a solicitor.'

'I see. So he was someone she bumped into on the path up to the grotto?'

'No, they walked to the grotto together because she wished to have a word with him. They had met before. A few times, in fact.'

'Mr Harris, you say? Never heard of him.'

'He has recently set up a solicitor firm in the village.'

'So why was she meeting with him?'

'Mr Campbell, there's no easy way of putting this, so I shall be direct.'

'Please do.'

'She was consulting the solicitor about a divorce.'

The detective's words hit him like a blow to the stomach.

'A divorce? No, never...' He rested his head in his hands and tried to take a breath. This news was a shock to him. He'd never realised Ruth had considered their marriage to be unhappy.

'You seem rather surprised by this news, Mr Campbell.'

'Surprised?' He sat up again. 'Of course I'm surprised. I thought we were in love! We were happy together for three years. After three failed marriages, I had finally met the woman I wanted to spend the rest of my life with. And now I discover she wanted to leave me! I can't believe she was thinking such thoughts shortly before she died. If only she could have spoken to me about the way she felt, and then we could have discussed it properly. But she died while feeling unhappy in our marriage. I shall never get over this!'

The detective sat back in his chair and puffed on his pipe. 'I should tell you what Mr Harris told me about his conversations with your late wife,' he said. 'She first approached him a couple of weeks ago to ask if she could discuss the possibility of divorce. At a second meeting, she explained to him she'd discovered her husband was having an affair.'

These words felt like a second punch.

'An affair?' He gasped. 'She thought I was having an affair? Oh, that's awful! If only I could explain myself to her. But I can't! Why didn't she tell me she thought these awful things about me? I could have set the record straight!'

'Were you having an affair?'

Mr Campbell fixed the detective's gaze, recalling Annie's words about detectives being well trained to spot liars. But it wasn't really an affair, was it? It was just a friendship.

'No,' he said.

'So you weren't having an affair with Annie Roberts?'

Once again, it took some time to recover from what the detective was saying.

'Annie Roberts?' He could hear his voice slightly choked as he said the name. 'I've never heard of her. Who is she?' His voice sounded weak now.

The detective puffed on his pipe, and Mr Campbell felt sure he wasn't fooling him at all.

'So you've never heard of Annie Roberts?'

It was useless to continue lying. He knew that the more he did it, the more ridiculous he looked.

'Oh, *Annie Roberts*? I think I misheard you the first time around.'

'What did you think I said?'

'I wasn't sure. I just didn't quite catch the name.'

'You didn't catch the name, and yet you said you'd never heard of her.'

He pulled out a handkerchief to show how distressed he

was. 'This is very difficult for me, Detective. My wife was murdered just a few days ago, and now I've discovered that she wished to divorce me. And now there are stories of me having an affair. This is all a lot to take in. I apologise if I'm not my normal self.'

'I understand, Mr Campbell. But the questions I'm asking you now are fairly simple. Were you having an affair with Annie Roberts?'

'We were friends.'

'You were friends?'

'Yes, we're not friends anymore, not since Ruth died. I was friendly with Annie, but she wanted more from it than I did. Actually, I was just about to tell her I didn't wish to be friendly with her at all when I heard the news that Ruth was dead.'

'So it was an affair that you were planning to end?'

'Yes, a very brief liaison which I'd decided had to end. I don't know how Ruth found out about it. I only wish she'd asked me about it because I could have reassured her it was nothing at all. Annie meant nothing to me.'

'Mr Harris informed me that your wife believed the affair had been continuing for almost two years.'

Mr Campbell didn't know what to do or say, so he laughed. 'Goodness, people must have been gossiping. All absolute nonsense, of course.'

'Two years?'

'I haven't exactly kept a record of when it began or when it ended. Perhaps there's a possibility it could have lasted almost that long. But it certainly didn't seem like it. And it meant nothing to me at all. Ruth was the true love of my life.'

'I'd like to make it clear that I'm not passing judgment on you, Mr Campbell. Ordinarily, what a man gets up to in his own time is no business of mine. But when we first met, you were keen to assure me how happy your marriage to your wife was. There was no mention of the affair at all. It is now my belief that you deliberately hid that information from me because it could have been a motive for murdering your wife.'

'Nonsense! I think it's quite obvious why I didn't admit the affair to you. I felt ashamed! I'm not proud of myself. I tried to keep it secret, and I didn't want anyone else to find out. But it couldn't possibly be a reason for murdering Ruth. What sort of man do you think I am?'

Chapter Thirty-Eight

AFTER LUNCH, Lottie and Rosie travelled by bus to Oswestry. The basket on her lap was filled with mince pies and a gift for Miss Beaufort at the orphanage. Rosie sat next to her, her nose twitching at the scent of fresh pastry. She made occasional attempts to poke her head into the basket, and Lottie had to give her a cautionary pat on the nose.

Was there anything more Miss Beaufort could tell her about the lady who'd asked after her? Lottie doubted it. But she was tired of visiting the library with a vague hope she might bump into the lady there. She had to do something more.

The path to the red brick orphanage had been cleared of snow. Lottie smiled at the many snowmen the children had built in the garden.

'Lottie!' Miss Beaufort welcomed her in the entrance hall. She had a French accent, wavy grey hair and smile lines at her eyes.

'The Christmas tree looks good this year,' said Lottie. It was decorated with shiny baubles and little gifts dangled from its branches. It was just as she remembered from her childhood. She could hear the excited chatter of the children from elsewhere in the building. Christmas had always been a special time at the orphanage with the staff and local people doing what they could for the children who lacked families to spend Christmas with.

Local farms had donated food for the Christmas dinner and people had brought in gifts for the children to unwrap. Lottie had always enjoyed Christmas here as a child.

Lottie handed her the basket. 'A gift for you and the children,' she said.

'Mince pies! Thank you very much, Lottie. Do I have to give these to the children, or can I eat them all myself?'

'I'll leave that decision to you,' said Lottie with a laugh.

'It's lovely to see your dog again,' she said, giving Rosie a pat. 'Come on through to the sitting room. I'll make us some tea.'

Lottie made herself comfortable on a sofa covered with a woollen blanket and cosy cushions. Rosie rested by her feet.

'I was so sorry to hear about poor Mrs Campbell,' said Miss Beaufort as she brought in the tea tray and placed it on a little table in front of the sofa. 'How could someone do something so awful? And to ruin the Christmas Fayre like that, too. It's worrying to think there's a murderer on the loose. Do the police have any idea who committed the crime?'

'From what I've heard, Mrs Campbell wasn't well liked. So there are a few people who might have held a grudge against her. Detective Inspector Lloyd is working on it and a detective from Scotland Yard will be on the way as soon as the railway line from London is cleared.'

They sipped their tea and talked a little about the Christmas plans for the orphanage. Then Lottie braved the question she'd been waiting to ask. 'I don't suppose she's returned, has she?'

'The lady who came here asking about you?' Miss Beaufort shook her head. 'I'm sorry, Lottie. She hasn't.'

'She must have been put off by Miss Spencer's words.'

'I think she probably was. I think it's a shame Miss Spencer doesn't believe in reuniting families. Her opinion is that it does more harm than good. I don't agree with her, which is why I mentioned the lady's visit to you, Lottie. I'm sorry you haven't been able to find her yet.'

'I've visited the library many times, hoping to see her. Do you believe she's local?'

'Yes, I feel quite sure of it. She had a local accent and told me she was going to take some books back to the library.'

'I wonder if there's a particular day of the week she visits the library. Can you recall what day of the week she visited?'

'It was a very rainy day, wasn't it?'

'Yes, I remember that. It was a good summer, but we had a week of quite bad weather,' Miss Beaufort confirmed.

'I can't recall when that was because I was away with Mrs Moore.'

'I think it was early June when we had that bad weather. Let me fetch my diary, maybe something will jog my memory.'

Miss Beaufort left the room and returned moments later with a small pocket diary. She sat in her armchair and leafed through it. 'Here we are,' she said. 'The first week of June. We'd planned to take the children on a day trip to Chirk Castle on Thursday the seventh, but I've crossed it out because we had to postpone it due to the weather. We took them the following week when the weather had improved again.'

'So that was during the week with the bad weather?' Lottie said. 'The week beginning the fourth of June?'

'Yes, it seems that must have been the case.'

'And did the lady visit on a weekday?' Lottie asked.

Miss Beaufort closed her eyes as she tried to recall. 'Yes, I believe it was a weekday, around lunchtime. I wasn't teaching lessons at that time. Actually, I can remember now! I think it was the Wednesday when she visited. We were discussing the bad weather and I remember telling her we'd had to cancel the trip for the following day. I feel sure it was the Wednesday.'

'So she was planning to go to the library on a Wednesday afternoon?'

'Yes. So perhaps you want to visit on a Wednesday? She might not go every Wednesday, though. Oh, I'm sorry, Lottie. I wish I'd asked her more questions! If I can remember any more detail which might help, I'll let you know.'

Today was Monday. Lottie resolved to visit the library again in two days' time.

Chapter Thirty-Nine

WALTER CAMPBELL TELEPHONED Annie as soon as the detective had left. 'Everything has gone horribly wrong. I've been interviewed by that detective again, and he's told me something quite shocking about Ruth.'

'Oh my goodness, what?'

'That man she was seen talking to shortly before she died was a solicitor. A Mr Harris. The gentleman is new to the area, which is why few people recognised him. Not only was she talking to him shortly before the attack, but she had also consulted him on a couple of occasions beforehand.'

'And you didn't know about this?'

'No! She didn't breathe a word of it to me. And it gets worse.'

'Why does it get worse?'

'Because apparently she was consulting him about a divorce.'

'Oh. But that's a good thing, isn't it? It shows she knew you weren't happy together anymore.'

He gritted his teeth. Annie had no idea how he felt! 'It's not a good thing, because she didn't mention it to me.'

'And you kept secrets from her too.'

'Well, I thought I did. But it turns out she knew about us.'

'She knew about us? How?'

'I don't know. Maybe Lily Granger said something to her. She saw us together that time, didn't she?'

'I don't believe she would have said anything.'

'So who did? Anyway, the long and the short of it is that Ruth knew about us and she wanted to get divorced. She was one step ahead of me. I can't tell you how awful it is to discover your deceased wife wished to divorce you. And now the detective knows you and I were having an affair. When I first spoke to him, I told him my marriage was happy. Now I look like a fool!'

'So why did you tell him that if it wasn't true?'

'Isn't it obvious? If I'd admitted our marriage wasn't happy, then I would have become a suspect, wouldn't I? But now it turns out I'm a suspect anyway, because the detective has found out I lied.'

'Detectives always find out these things, Walter. I've told you that. Oh, I can't bear the thought that Ruth knew I was having an affair with her husband! I thought she looked at me rather coldly, but I assumed that was her nature. But to think she actually knew all along that we were having an affair. Well, it's embarrassing, isn't it?'

'And it won't be long before everyone knows, Annie. The detective knows, the solicitor knows, Lily Granger knows... it's a complete and utter mess. I just know they're going to arrest me.'

'Why will they arrest you?'

'Because it looks like we plotted to get rid of her, doesn't it?'

'*We*? Why does this have anything to do with me?'

'You know how the mind of a detective works, Annie,

you've explained it to me enough times. He's going to blame both of us.'

'But he can't! He can't blame me as well!'

'Oh, he can, and he probably will. So watch out, Annie. That detective is going to come for you, too.'

THERE WAS a knock on Lottie's bedroom door as she got ready for dinner that evening.

'Come in!'

Mildred fell into the room, her face pale. 'Oh Lottie, come and see this!'

'What is it?'

'I'll show you,' she replied. She dashed off again, and Lottie and Rosie followed her down three flights of service stairs to the basement. There, they made their way through the corridors to the laundry room.

'Not the secret tunnel?' said Lottie, jogging to keep up with Mildred's brisk pace.

'No. But almost.'

Mildred walked over to the sinks and the stack of wash tubs which Mr Duxbury had moved out of the storage room with the trapdoor.

'It occurred to me we didn't search the laundry room properly after we found the secret tunnel,' she said. 'I had some time to spare, so I thought I'd look around and then I found... well, have a look.'

'At what?'

'Lift up that top washing tub.'

Lottie did so. And as she looked in the tub beneath it, a cold shiver ran down her spine.

Inside the tub was a gun.

'Oh, good grief,' said Lottie. 'It's the weapon, isn't it?' Lottie wasn't familiar with guns, but she knew enough to guess this one was a pistol or revolver. 'Who have you told about this, Mildred?'

'No one yet. It frightened me! We should tell Miss Hudson and Mr Duxbury, shouldn't we?'

'Yes, we should. You haven't touched it, have you?'

'No.'

'The police will need to dust it for fingerprints. I'm amazed this gun wasn't found sooner. Why didn't we find it when we moved the tubs out of the storage room?'

'Mr Duxbury just picked them up in one go, do you remember? We were too busy thinking about the trapdoor to look inside them.'

'So this must be Mr Palmer's gun,' said Lottie.

'Yes. And Mrs Palmer must have put it there. Now we know why she wanted to stay away from the secret tunnel. She knew about the gun being hidden here! She didn't want to be around when it was found. And I swear she's up to something. Do you remember me telling you I saw her in the corridor with a bag in her hand? And when she saw me, she turned around and went the other way. Well, I've seen her a few more times now. I don't know where she goes or what the bag is for. It's usually in the morning, once breakfast is finished. And before she starts preparing lunch. Perhaps I could follow her?'

'I think that's a good idea. But be careful she doesn't spot you. In the meantime, we need to tell someone about this gun.'

A short while later, the household staff gathered in the laundry room and peered at the gun in the wash tub.

'Let me have a look,' said Mrs Palmer, striding over to them. She surveyed the weapon for a moment. 'One gun looks much like another, really, doesn't it? But I'd say that looks like my husband's gun. How did it end up in a wash tub?'

Chapter Forty-One

DINNER WAS DELAYED that evening while Detective Inspector Lloyd carried out his investigations. He then gathered the household in the drawing room. A short, wide man with a face like a bulldog joined them. Lottie guessed he was Mr Palmer.

'By now you'll all be aware that a Webley revolver has been found in a wash tub in the laundry room,' said the detective. 'A few days ago, Mr Palmer here reported his gun missing. I've shown him the gun found in the wash tub and he's confirmed it belongs to him.'

'It's nice to have it back,' said Mr Palmer.

'I'm afraid you can't have it back,' said the detective. 'I highly suspect your gun is a murder weapon. It needs to be examined and I'm hoping we'll get some useful fingerprints from it.'

'It will have my fingerprints on it!'

'Yes it will, Mr Palmer. And obviously we'll discount those. We're looking for the murderer's prints.'

'So how did the gun end up in the laundry room?' asked Lady Buckley-Phipps.

'Let's not waste the detective's time with pointless questions, Lucinda,' said her husband. 'It's quite obvious, isn't it? The murderer hid it in a wash tub after returning to the house via the secret tunnel.'

'So the murderer was in the house?'

'Yes, I suppose they must have been. It's not a nice thought.'

Detective Inspector Lloyd puffed on his pipe, then turned to the cook. 'I'd like to have a word with you in the music room, please, Mrs Palmer.'

'Me? Why?'

'Because I would like to understand a little more about your relationship with Mrs Campbell.'

'Relationship? We didn't have one! I worked for the Campbells for a few weeks and then she fired me!'

'All the same, I would like a word.'

Chapter Forty-Two

HANNAH PALMER SAT in a chair opposite Detective Inspector Lloyd in the music room. Her tummy rumbled. Usually the servants would be eating now, after having served dinner to the Buckley-Phipps family. She folded her arms and watched the detective consult his notebook.

'Your husband's gun went missing at around the time of Mrs Campbell's murder.'

'That's right. And if you're suggesting I took it, Detective, I didn't.'

'It was found in the laundry room. A room in this house which is connected by a tunnel to the grotto.'

'So I've heard.'

He sat back in his chair and puffed on his pipe. 'Were you aware of the secret tunnel, Mrs Palmer?'

'No. I never knew the first thing about it. No one did, from what I've heard.'

'The murderer did.'

'How do you know that?'

'Because he or she used the tunnel to access the grotto.'

'And how do you know they did that?'

'Because the murder weapon was found in a wash tub in the laundry room.'

'How do you know it's the murder weapon?'

The detective scowled. 'I'm the one who's supposed to be asking the questions, Mrs Palmer. Your husband's revolver is a Webley Mark V. Exactly the same type used in the murder of Mrs Campbell. We know this from analysis of the bullets found at the scene.'

'But there are loads of Webley revolvers around, Detective. They were used in the war and lots of men brought them home.'

'True. But there are too many coincidences here for me not to be on the right track.'

'But a coincidence is a coincidence, Detective. You've got no proof I'm involved in any of this. And you're keeping me from my evening meal.'

Hannah had no time for anyone who got between her and her food.

'Let's take each piece of evidence in turn, shall we?'

'Evidence? I don't think you have any.'

'First of all, you were employed by Mr and Mrs Campbell earlier this year. Is that right?'

'Yes, that's right.'

'And how long did you work for them?'

'Just over three weeks.'

'A short tenure. May I ask why you worked for them for just a few weeks?'

'Mrs Campbell didn't like me.'

'She told you that?'

'Not quite so directly, but it was obvious. She dismissed me because she told me I couldn't cook. I know I can cook because I've been a cook for years. I was cooking dinners for the finest families in Shropshire when she was still throwing dollies out of her perambulator. But Mrs Campbell clearly took a dislike to me and used the excuse I couldn't cook just to get rid of me.'

'Why didn't you mention this to Lady Buckley-Phipps when she took you on as the cook here at Fortescue Manor?'

'Because I felt ashamed about it. I've explained that to her ladyship, and she understands. I know she's very happy with my work here.'

'You must have been angry when you were dismissed after such a short period of time. And also angry to be accused of being unable to cook.'

'It was an upsetting experience, but I wouldn't say I was angry. In fact, I view it now as a good thing. I couldn't have carried on working for a lady who didn't like me, could I? It would have been no fun at all. So the fact she dismissed me was better for me in the long run.'

'It's understandable that you could have borne Mrs Campbell a grudge.'

'Maybe I could have. If I was that sort of person. But life's too short to bear grudges, Detective.' This wasn't a belief she lived by, but she thought it sounded good. 'And I knew Mrs Campbell was an unpopular lady and was rude to people. So she paid for it in the end, didn't she? It's often the way, Detective. And a lesson for us all. Always treat others how you wish to be treated yourself.'

'You didn't seek revenge for how she'd treated you?'

'No. I'm not the sort of person to seek revenge. Life's too short for that, too.'

'How do you explain your husband's gun going missing around the time of the murder?'

'I can't explain it. And knowing him, he's probably mislaid it somewhere.'

'Accidentally mislaid a loaded gun?'

'I wouldn't be surprised.'

'Has he done that before?'

'No, but there's always a first time, isn't there?'

'Are you the person who took his gun, Mrs Palmer?'

'No! I have no interest in guns.'

'Who else could have taken it?'

'I don't know. We never lock our door so, in theory, anyone could have wandered in and taken it. They would had to have known it was there, though.'

'Who knew it was there?'

'I don't know. My husband might be able to tell you.'

'Could he have wished to murder Mrs Campbell?'

'He barely knew her.'

'Perhaps he was angry that she dismissed you from your job?'

'Yes, he was angry about it. But not so angry that he would have shot her. He wouldn't have done that at all. And besides, how would he have known about the secret tunnel and put his gun in the wash tub in the laundry room?'

'Maybe he asked you to dispose of the weapon for him?'

'Impossible, Detective.'

'As far as I can see, Mrs Palmer, you're the only person who could have easily fetched the gun from your home and then placed it in the wash tub in the laundry room. I think you had time to dash through that secret tunnel, commit the crime and get back to the house before anyone noticed you were missing.'

Hannah gave a laugh. 'And even if I was that clever, Detective, how would I have known Mrs Campbell would be in the grotto at that time?'

'You arranged to meet her there.'

Chapter Forty-Three

WALTER CAMPBELL CALLED at the offices of Harris Solicitors in Lowton Chorley the following morning. A sign on the secretary's desk said, *Merry Christmas to all our Clients!* Walter scowled and addressed the bespectacled secretary behind the desk. 'Mr Harris please.'

'Do you have an appointment, sir?'

'No.'

'Then I'm afraid—'

'I'm Mr Campbell, the mayor of Oswestry. Just tell him I wish to discuss my late wife, Ruth Campbell.'

Moments later, Walter sat opposite a smart, fair-haired gentleman who looked too young to be a decent solicitor. His smart office was furnished with mahogany furniture, and a twinkling Christmas tree stood by the window.

'Please accept my most sincere condolences on the passing of your wife,' said Mr Harris.

'I'd like to find out what she discussed with you.'

'I shall tell you what I can, Mr Campbell. However, I abide by confidentiality.'

'Confidentiality? But Ruth was my wife, and she's no longer here. So why must there be confidentiality?'

'It's how we conduct things here at Harris Solicitors, Mr Campbell.'

'*We*? As far as I can see, it's only you and a secretary here. A small operation, from what I can tell.'

'We have a sister office in Oswestry with four solicitors.'

'I see.'

'And another office in Shrewsbury with eight.'

Walter gave a snort and adjusted his jacket. 'Very well. I understand my wife consulted you about divorcing me.'

'I'm not at liberty to—'

'Now come along, I know she did because Detective Inspector Lloyd told me so. And I understand she was considering a divorce because she had learned of my infidelity.'

'Yes.'

'Do you know how?'

'I understand an acquaintance told her.'

'Do you know which acquaintance?'

'She didn't share the name of the person.'

'Mrs Lily Granger?'

'I don't know. She didn't say.'

'I need to know who it was.'

'May I ask why? Now that your wife has passed away, I'm not sure anything can be gained by finding out who it was, can it?'

'I suppose not. How serious was she about the divorce?'

'Very serious.'

'So she was definitely going to go ahead with it?'

The solicitor nodded.

'Good grief.' Walter's stomach tied into a knot. All the

kindness she'd shown him during the last few weeks of her life had been an act. She'd been planning to leave him all along.

'Did she mention to you when she was going to tell me about this?'

'She was waiting for me to finish the papers, and then she was going to hand them to you. So, I imagine it would have been within the next week.'

'Right. So that would have been that. What did you discuss at the Christmas Fayre?'

'Mrs Campbell was eager to find out when the papers would be ready. She'd wanted to inform you about the divorce before Christmas.'

'Before Christmas?' He felt his jaw drop. 'Did she still want to spend Christmas with me?'

'I really couldn't say, Mr Campbell.'

Ruth had been planning to ruin his Christmas! She really hadn't cared about him at all.

'I wish I'd had the chance to explain things to her,' he said. 'If I'd known she'd found out about the affair, then we could have discussed it and reached a solution.' He pointed a finger at the solicitor. 'You shouldn't have let it go this far, Harris. You should have told me what she was planning!'

'I was under no obligation whatsoever to inform you, Mr Campbell. Perhaps you should have thought about the repercussions of an extramarital affair before you embarked on it.'

'So it's my fault?'

'You strike me as a clever man, Mr Campbell. I advise you to reflect on your actions and reach your own conclusion.'

He got up from his seat. 'I find your manner impertinent. You do realise you're speaking to a mayor?'

'Yes.'

To Walter's annoyance, the solicitor calmly checked his watch, as if bored by the conversation.

'One more question,' said Walter. 'Who was the friend my wife had arranged to meet in the grotto?'

'I don't know.'

'But there was definitely an arrangement?'

'Yes.'

'And she didn't tell you the name?'

'No. Did she mention the arrangement to you?'

'No, she didn't. So you could be making it up!'

'Why would I do that, Mr Campbell?'

'Because you could be the murderer! You could be making up a story about Ruth meeting a friend when it was you who committed the crime! You might fool Detective Inspector Lloyd, but you don't fool me!'

DETECTIVE INSPECTOR LLOYD made an unexpected appearance in the breakfast room at Fortescue Manor.

'I apologise for the interruption, my lord,' he said to Lord Buckley-Phipps. 'But I need to inform you I've just arrested your cook, Mrs Palmer.'

'What?' Lord Buckley-Phipps dropped his fork. 'You've arrested her for murder?'

'Yes, my lord.'

'On what grounds?'

'She murdered Ruth Campbell in revenge for her dismissal.'

'I can't imagine Mrs Palmer doing such a thing!' said Mrs Moore.

'Neither can I,' said Barty.

'Not only did she have a motive for murdering Mrs Campbell, but she was well placed to carry out the crime,' said the detective. 'She took her husband's revolver and used the tunnel between the house and the grotto to swiftly get to and from the scene of the crime.'

'She knew about the tunnel?' said Barty.

'She must have done.'

'But how did she know about it when no one else did?'

'She's yet to explain that to me, but I'll get it out of her soon enough.'

'And how did she know Mrs Campbell was going to be in the grotto?' said Mrs Moore.

'She arranged to meet her there.'

'Is that what Mrs Palmer has told you?'

'No, but the solicitor, Mr Harris, said Mrs Campbell had arranged to meet a friend at the grotto. That friend must have been Mrs Palmer.'

'You have evidence of this?' asked Lord Buckley-Phipps.

'Not yet, my lord. But that's another thing I'll get out of her soon enough.'

'And it was Mrs Palmer who put her husband's gun in the wash tub?' asked Mrs Moore.

'Yes, madam. As soon as she returned from the crime, via the tunnel, she hid the murder weapon in one of the empty wash tubs.'

'You've found her fingerprints on it?' asked Mrs Moore.

'Not yet. But I anticipate we will.'

'Well, I suppose the arrest is good news,' said Lord Buckley-Phipps. 'But it's an awful shame the culprit is a member of the household staff. And the cook too! It's going to be tricky to hire a decent replacement this side of Christmas. Lucinda's not going to be happy about it at all.'

Lottie didn't know what to make of this news. Although there were reasons to suspect Mrs Palmer, there didn't appear to be any firm evidence against her.

'I suppose I should say well done, Detective,' said Lord Buckley-Phipps. 'Now that the culprit has been arrested, we can have a peaceful and joyful Christmas!'

'Yes, well done,' said Mrs Moore, raising her cup of tea in a toast. 'How nice to have it all resolved.'

Chapter Forty-Five

'I'M NOT LOOKING FORWARD to lunchtime,' said Mildred. 'With Mrs Palmer gone, I've got to help Miss Hudson with the cooking.'

They stood in the library where Mildred was wafting her feather duster over the shelves.

'Do you think Mrs Palmer is a murderer?' Lottie asked.

'I don't know. Do you?'

'I don't know either.'

'I saw her yesterday in the corridor with her bag,' said Mildred. 'And I managed to see where she went.'

'Where?'

'To the door at the end of the corridor near the gun room and boot room.'

'I remember that door,' said Lottie. 'No one uses it, do they? I thought it led outside.'

'Yes, I thought so too.'

'But why would she go through that door when she can easily get to the servants' courtyard from the kitchen?' said Lottie.

'I don't know, and it's been such a long time since I went through that door that I can't remember if it leads directly outside or if there's another storeroom there. Maybe there's even another secret passageway.'

'Well, there's only one way to find out, isn't there?' said Lottie. 'We need to go through the door and find out why she's so keen on it.'

'I tried the door earlier, and it's locked. I'm sure the key will be in Miss Hudson's office. I need you to act as a lookout for me, Lottie, while I fetch it.'

'Alright, let's try it now.'

Lottie, Rosie and Mildred made their way to the housekeeper's office. Fortunately, there was no sign of Miss Hudson. Lottie and Rosie stood in the corridor, keeping watch as Mildred went to look for the key.

Jack passed by. 'Hello, Miss Sprigg.'

'Hello Jack.' She felt her face blush.

He paused and glanced around. 'Are you waiting for someone?'

'Yes. I'm waiting for Mildred. Sad news about Mrs Palmer, isn't it?'

'Yes, that surprised me. When I saw her knitting in the servants' hall that afternoon, she looked like she'd been sitting there for some time. It's difficult to believe she'd just carried out a murder. Perhaps she's just good at fooling people. You'd have to be to do something like that.'

'I agree. And it's possible the detective is mistaken.'

'Perhaps he just wants to arrest someone so he can solve the case before Christmas.'

Lottie laughed. 'I can imagine that being the truth!'

Mildred appeared. 'Sorry to interrupt,' she said.

'You're not interrupting anything,' said Lottie.

'No nothing,' said Jack. He said goodbye and went on his way.

'I should have spent more time looking for the key so you could have chatted to him some more,' said Mildred as they continued on down the corridor.

'No, you shouldn't have,' said Lottie. 'Now let's investigate this door before anyone else notices us.' She strode on ahead, leaving Mildred to catch up.

They proceeded down the corridor, passed a staircase, the sewing room, the laundry room, and the gun room. 'I saw Mrs Palmer try the handle of the gun room door,' said Mildred. 'Maybe she was just checking it was locked?'

'Odd.' Lottie tried the handle. 'It's still locked. I wonder why she checked it. There are too many unanswered questions.'

'But hopefully we're about to find an answer by opening this door,' said Mildred. They reached the end of the corridor and she put the key into the lock. She turned it and the door pulled inwards.

They were met by a gust of cold air and the bright light of sunshine on snow.

'I remember this now,' said Mildred. The door opened onto a little paved area with steps that led up to the gardens at the side of the house. Rosie trotted past them and sniffed about. 'What's been happening here?'

Hundreds of little prints had disturbed the snow. Lottie stepped outside to examine them. 'Birds?' she said.

'And something else, too,' said Mildred, pointing to the top of the steps. A little squirrel observed them, its head cocked to one side. A robin landed close by and Rosie was too distracted by the scents in the snow to notice it.

'It's as if they're waiting for something,' said Lottie.

'Food,' said Mildred.

'Do you think that's what Mrs Palmer had in her bag? Food for the wildlife?'

Mildred nodded. 'She must have been feeling sorry for them with all this snow on the ground.'

'I feel bad we've got nothing for them,' said Lottie as another squirrel appeared.

'Mrs Palmer must have kept it quiet because his lordship has been complaining about the vermin,' said Mildred. 'We'd been told not to put out any food because it encourages the rats.'

'So that's why she was being so secretive,' said Lottie.

'It's very nice of her to feed the animals,' said Mildred.

'I agree,' said Lottie. She called Rosie back to the house, and they went back inside.

'Now we've discovered what she was up to, it's difficult to believe she could be a murderer,' said Mildred as she locked the door behind them.

'What are you two up to?' came Miss Hudson's voice down the corridor.

Mildred quickly responded, 'We had a few food scraps, so we threw them out onto the terrace.'

'Food scraps? You shouldn't be throwing them outside!' The housekeeper stood in the corridor, her hands on her hips.

'I'm sorry. We won't do it again, Miss Hudson,' said Mildred.

'I should hope not!' The housekeeper turned to Lottie. 'I'm sorry I scolded you, Miss Sprigg. I suppose I'm used to it from when you were a maid. I think Mrs Moore would be disappointed if she knew you were encouraging the vermin.'

'We didn't see any vermin,' said Lottie. 'Just a robin and two squirrels, who are probably hungry while all this snow is on the ground.'

The housekeeper sighed, then lowered her voice. 'Fine. But at the first sign of any rats, you'll have to stop. Does that sound fair? And if you want the key, just ask for it. Don't go taking it without permission. Now come along, Mildred. You need to help me prepare lunch.'

Chapter Forty-Six

ANNIE ROBERTS SAT in her armchair with a velvet-covered gift box in her hand. She lifted its lid and examined the beautiful watch nestling on a satin cushion inside. This was supposed to be her Christmas gift for Walter. But now she was uncertain what to do with it. Should she give it to him? Or should she return it to the jewellers and get her money back?

Walter had told her the detective was coming for her as well as him. It wasn't a comforting thing to say. Had he been deliberately trying to frighten her? If so, it was a mean thing to do.

She recalled Lily Granger saying Walter had once propositioned her, and she'd batted him away. At the time, Annie had been determined to disbelieve it. But could it be true? Walter had once told her he'd had other affairs in the past. Perhaps he was the sort of man who enjoyed getting attention from as many ladies as possible.

Annie suspected Lily Granger had told Ruth Campbell about the affair. It was embarrassing to think Ruth had known about them, but it was a shame she hadn't considered divorce sooner. If she had, then Annie and Walter would have been free to be together. She could have spent Christmas with the man she loved.

Or could she? Walter was upset to learn Ruth had wished to divorce him. Did that mean he'd never intended to leave his wife after all? Presumably he'd wanted to continue having an affair while also pretending to be happily married. Despite all his assurances, Annie was probably only ever destined to be his mistress. And likely to be replaced by a new one before long.

She had been so foolish! She closed the gift box and put it on the table next to her chair. Walter didn't deserve the watch. She would be better off returning it and using the money to spend on herself.

Despite the turmoil of the past five days, Annie found solace in one thing. She'd successfully prevented Lily Granger from taking control of the Lowton Chorley Ladies' Society. And now she could stand against her and have a chance of winning the vote herself. She felt determined now to do whatever she could to become the chair of the Ladies' Society. Defeating Lily Granger was her goal. If she could manage it, it would be her Christmas present to herself. And she would prove to Walter Campbell what she could achieve without him.

Chapter Forty-Seven

LILY GRANGER TIPPED the ball of pastry onto the floured worktop and picked up her rolling pin. She was pleased with how the pastry had turned out. She had always been good at making pastry. It was light and crumbly, but not too crumbly. It was never tough and tasteless like pastry made by others she knew. She hummed a Christmas tune to herself as she dusted some flour onto her rolling pin. Then she rolled out the ball into a flat circle.

Becoming chair of the Lowton Chorley Ladies' Society had been an ambition of hers for many years. She'd done her best to ingratiate herself with every single member of the group, even though she found many of them insufferable. She'd worked diligently at every fundraising event, attended all the meetings, and organised all the activities which other people didn't want to do. She couldn't have worked any harder.

She took a sip of sherry, then cut out little circles of pastry. Twelve large circles and twelve smaller ones. Then she placed each large pastry circle into the round moulds of the baking tray, easing each one into place with a gentle press of her forefinger.

She smiled as she recalled the moment of sheer joy when she'd been shortlisted in the contest to become chair. She'd been certain she would get more votes than Ruth Campbell, so it had been disappointing to have the vote tied between them.

She picked up her bowl of mincemeat and gave it a sniff. It was richly fruited, with a good dose of brandy in it too. She hummed another Christmas tune as she spooned the mixture into each mince pie base.

She had probably underestimated Ruth as a competitor. Despite being unpopular, Ruth had been known for getting things done. And her status in the local community had grown with her husband's appointment as mayor. People hadn't liked her much, but they had seen her as someone with influence. How could Lily Granger, even after all her hard work, compete with that?

Now Lily had Annie Roberts to contend with. Who could possibly want to vote for her? Everyone felt sorry for her, taken in by Walter Campbell's charms. What an odious man he was! It was a shame he hadn't been murdered too.

After spooning out all the mincemeat, Lily wiped her hands on her apron and proudly surveyed her work. Then she went to her scullery, took out a small box of rat poison, and returned to the kitchen. She opened the box, picked up a teaspoon, dipped it onto the poison and sprinkled a small amount on top of the mixture in one of the mince pies. She mixed it into the mincemeat a little to disguise it. Sometimes people removed the lids of their mince pies, and she didn't want that happening.

Then she placed the small pastry circles on top of the mincemeat so each mince pie had a little lid. She picked up a fork and poked three holes with its prongs into each lid. When she reached the mince pie with the rat poison in it, she pricked the lid twice to make six little holes. Now she knew which mince pie was the one for Annie.

She glazed the mince pies with a slick of egg white so they would turn a beautiful brown.

Just as she was about to put the mince pies into the oven, there was a knock at the door. She pulled off her apron, smoothed her hair and went to answer it.

'This is a surprise,' she said, as she saw who was standing there. 'What do you want?'

They were the last words she ever said.

Chapter Forty-Eight

'QUITE SHOCKING,' said Mrs Moore once she'd read the report of the murder in the newspaper the following morning. 'Why would someone attack Lily Granger?'

'I've no idea,' said Lord Buckley-Phipps. 'It's an absolute scandal.'

'It's awful!' said his wife. 'The killer has struck again!'

'Perhaps it's someone from the Lowton Chorley Ladies' Society,' said Mrs Moore. 'They got rid of Mrs Campbell, and now they've got rid of Mrs Granger too. It must be something to do with the power struggle to become chair.'

'But it's no way to settle a power struggle, is it?' said Barty.

'I've often said these ladies' groups are far more ruthless than anything gentlemen get up to,' said Lord Buckley-Phipps. 'Watch out Barty. Never court a lady who's a member of one of those groups.'

'Oh stop talking nonsense, Ivan,' said Lady Buckley-Phipps. 'Those ladies aren't any worse or any better than anyone else. It's just a terrible tragedy.'

'So what exactly happened?' Lottie asked. She hadn't had the chance to look at the newspaper yet.

'It says here that neighbours heard a gunshot at around two o'clock yesterday afternoon,' said Mrs Moore. 'A neighbour dashed out of her house and realised the shot had come from Lily Granger's house next door. The front door was standing open, but there was no sign of anyone about. She stepped into the hallway and saw poor Mrs Granger lying on the floor.'

'Dreadful,' said Barty.

'The killer has got away again,' said Mrs Moore. 'They clearly knocked at the door, and when Mrs Granger answered it, they carried out the dreadful deed.'

'So why Mrs Granger?' said Barty. 'Perhaps she knew who Ruth Campbell's killer was and was silenced? Or perhaps the killer was someone who thought she'd murdered Ruth Campbell and was seeking revenge?'

'Who knows what the reason is, Barty?' said his father. 'I've already referred to the ruthless nature of the ladies involved and have been slapped down by your mother. It's something for the police to work out.'

'I can't imagine there are many clues to go on,' said Mrs Moore. 'The murderer appears to have run away without being spotted. Detective Inspector Lloyd is going to have his work cut out with this one.'

'But it's not necessarily the same murderer, is it?' said Barty.

'Perhaps not,' said Mrs Moore. 'But the method of murder was the same, wasn't it? A gun.'

'We found the gun from the first murder, and now there's a second gun being used,' Lord Buckley-Phipps noted. 'Who's getting hold of all these guns?'

'It could be a gamekeeper,' said Barty. 'But it can't be Mrs Palmer the cook because she's in police custody.'

'Good point, Barty!' said Lord Buckley-Phipps. 'She can't possibly have carried out this murder. And that makes me wonder if she's innocent of Ruth Campbell's murder too! I suspect Detective Inspector Lloyd has arrested the wrong person. Thankfully the detective from the Yard should be here soon. It says in the paper this morning that the railway line has been cleared and the trains will be running again.'

'You'll be able to get to your Buckingham Palace Christmas ball, Roberta!' said Lady Buckley-Phipps.

'Golly. I'd almost forgotten about that. How exciting! It's just two days' away! We'd better start packing today, Lottie.'

Chapter Forty-Nine

LOTTIE SPENT the morning arranging the trip to London. She telephoned the railway station to book their train tickets and began packing their cases. Mrs Moore hadn't yet decided which outfit to wear to the ball, so Lottie had to carefully fold and pack various gowns.

'I need to go to the library this afternoon to return my books,' she said to Mrs Moore.

'Of course, Lottie. And don't forget there's a lovely little library in Chelsea where you can borrow some new books to read.'

Lottie didn't want to spend Christmas in London. She wanted to stay at Fortescue Manor. Although she felt excited about visiting Buckingham Palace, she knew she would feel out of place there. She pictured a vast ballroom decorated in white and gold and filled with the great and good of the country. Lottie imagined herself standing at the edge of the room, not knowing who to speak to. She didn't even know how to dance. She'd been shown a few steps at a masquerade ball in Venice, but that was all.

* * *

'Back again, Miss Sprigg?' said Annie Roberts, the librarian. 'You read those books quickly.'

'I enjoy reading,' said Lottie. 'Although the past week has been more eventful than anything you can find in a detective story.'

Miss Roberts sighed. 'It has indeed. It's terrible. I don't believe the Lowton Chorley Ladies' Society will ever recover. The two ladies who had hoped to be chair of our group have both been murdered! I don't understand it at all. Between you and me, I wondered if Lily had murdered Ruth. I know that sounds rather judgemental of me, but they didn't like each other. I noticed them engrossed in heated conversation a couple of times before Ruth's death.'

'Do you know what they were discussing?'

'I'm sure I heard money mentioned. And Lily mentioned her son Philip, too. Although I don't know what he had to do with it.'

'So not only were Mrs Campbell and Mrs Granger rivals for the position of chair, but there was a disagreement about money too?'

'That was my impression. But I could be mistaken.'

'And you thought Mrs Granger had murdered Mrs Campbell?'

'It was an idea I had. Although I don't know the full details of their disagreement, Lily seemed consumed by ambition and possibly thought that getting rid of Ruth would allow her to become the chair. That was one of the reasons why I stood up to her and insisted we all vote again.'

Lottie recalled the conversation she'd heard between Annie and Walter Campbell when she was last in the library.

'Am I right in thinking you put yourself forward as chair after the death of Ruth Campbell?'

'Oh. You heard about that? Yes, I did. I can't deny I had ambitions for the role myself.'

'So that's the real reason you stood up to her?'

'No, not just for that reason. I didn't think it was fair Lily should be chair because only half of the group voted for her.'

'Do you think someone from the Ladies' Society is behind these murders?'

Miss Roberts gave this some thought, possibly wondering how to answer without implicating herself. 'It could have been someone from the Ladies' Society,' she said. 'Perhaps someone who didn't want Ruth or Lily to become chair. And maybe they thought a simple solution would be to get rid of both of them. Of course, it's not a simple solution, it's murder! And when this person gets caught, they're going to be in an awful lot of trouble about it.'

'Did you like Mrs Granger?' Lottie asked.

Annie Roberts gave an awkward laugh. 'What a question! We weren't friends, and she certainly took a dislike to me after I stopped her from taking the role of chair. She threatened me, in fact.'

'Really?'

'Sorry, no she didn't.' Annie clearly realised she'd said too much. 'She was unpleasant to me, but she didn't threaten me.'

'So why did you say she had?'

'It was a mistake. Anyway, I must be getting on, Miss Sprigg.' She fixed a false smile on her face.

'Yes,' said Lottie. 'Just one more thing. Do you still have ambitions to become the chair of the Ladies' Society, Miss Roberts?'

'No. Just look at what's happened to the two ladies who put themselves forward! As I've said, I don't think the Ladies' Society can recover from this. Sadly, Miss Sprigg, I think it might need to be disbanded.'

· · ·

Rosie wagged her tail as Lottie joined her outside the library.

'I don't know what to make of Miss Roberts,' she whispered to her dog. 'Has she just told me the truth? Or was it all a pack of lies?'

She stopped talking to her dog as she noticed a lady climbing the library steps with a basket in her hand. Her clothes were plain and unremarkable, but there was something about her face that struck Lottie as familiar. She felt as though she'd seen her before, but she also felt sure she hadn't. It was an odd sensation, and she wondered if she had finally seen the lady who'd asked about her at the orphanage.

'Rosie,' she said to the corgi. 'I'm going to have to ask you to remain here a little longer, I'm afraid. I know it's cold, but I'll be as quick as I can.'

She stepped back into the library where the lady was returning some books to Miss Roberts at the desk.

Was the lady familiar? Lottie didn't feel so sure now. She walked to the detective stories section, where she could pretend to browse.

After a moment, she peered around the bookcase and saw the lady walking towards her.

Lottie felt she should know her. There was something in the shape of her eyes and the line of her nose that was familiar. But she didn't want to stare too much. And perhaps it was just wishful thinking. Maybe she'd been waiting for so long to find the woman who'd asked about her that she was now pinning her hopes on a lady of similar appearance.

The lady began browsing the detective stories just a few yards from where Lottie stood. Hadn't Miss Beaumont said she'd spotted a detective book in the lady's basket?

This had to be the same lady.

Lottie's heart thudded heavily in her chest. She pulled out

a book and leafed through it without looking at any of the words. Her hands were trembling. Should she say something to the woman? They clearly both liked detective stories. Perhaps that would be a way of starting a conversation?

Lottie took a breath, preparing herself. She would perhaps ask the woman for a recommendation. She would ask her to tell her what her favourite book was.

She took in another breath, preparing to speak, but then the silence was broken.

'Josephine!' came a whisper from behind Lottie.

'Hello, Susan,' she whispered with a smile.

As she turned to her friend, Josephine's eyes met Lottie's. For a brief moment, they held each other's gaze.

Had she recognised something about Lottie, too?

Susan walked past Lottie, blocking their view of each other. She began to talk in a hushed voice about her failed attempt at making a Christmas cake and Lottie realised her opportunity was lost.

A little bark from outside told her that Rosie was cold and tired from waiting.

Reluctantly, Lottie left the library.

But all was not lost.

She knew the lady's name.

Chapter Fifty

'Mrs Palmer the cook has returned,' Mrs Moore told Lottie as she and Rosie joined her in the sitting room for afternoon tea. 'Detective Inspector Lloyd released her from custody this morning. Lucinda has told her she can take the day off, but apparently she's downstairs telling everyone all about her stay in the police cell.'

'So the detective is certain she's innocent?'

'Apparently so. She can't possibly have murdered Lily Granger, so he thinks she's innocent of Ruth Campbell's murder, too. And just yesterday, he was convinced she was guilty! Hopefully, the Scotland Yard detective will sort it out. Ivan says he's due to arrive this evening. I realise this case is something you would have liked to have solved, Lottie, but I'm afraid we must depart for London tomorrow.'

Lottie nodded, trying to hide her disappointment. 'Perhaps I'm just being nosy, but I think I'll go downstairs and hear what Mrs Palmer has to say.'

'Yes, by all means! You can report back to me, Lottie. I'm nosy too.'

. . .

Lottie found Mrs Palmer and most of the servants in the servants' hall.

'I think everyone should spend a night in a cell,' said the cook. 'Only then can you fully appreciate what you have in life.'

'I would go mad!' said Mildred.

'I think I appreciate what I have in life without being locked in a cell,' said the housekeeper.

'That's what I thought, Miss Hudson,' said the cook. 'But being locked up puts a different slant on it altogether. Your mind goes to places you can't ever have imagined.'

'Good grief,' said Mr Duxbury.

'And it's worse when you're completely innocent,' continued Mrs Palmer. 'You know you've done nothing wrong and yet there you are being punished. For no reason at all! That detective really is completely hopeless.'

'Detective Inspector Lloyd was under pressure to make an arrest,' said Miss Hudson. 'And now he's made himself look foolish.'

'He has. If he'd arrested the right person, then Lily Granger would still be alive! My husband is desperately upset.'

'Your husband's upset?' asked the housekeeper. 'Why?'

'Because Lily Granger was his sister,' said Mrs Palmer.

'Goodness, I never knew that! Please accept my condolences. And if you would like more time off—'

'There's no need,' the cook interrupted. 'Lily and I weren't close. My husband, Peter, is getting on with his work today because he doesn't want to be sitting around moping about it. All we can do is hope the detective catches this dreadful killer.'

'I'm sorry to hear you and your sister-in-law didn't get on, Mrs Palmer,' said Lottie.

'She never liked me very much because she thought her brother could have married someone better. Disapproving of other people was a hobby of hers. Peter will miss her and I'll pretend to miss her for his sake.'

Mildred caught up with Lottie after she left the servants' hall. 'What time is your train tomorrow?' she asked.

'Midday. I think we need to leave at eleven o'clock.'

'So I'll have time to say goodbye to you first thing. You don't look very happy about going to London, Lottie.'

'I'm not really. I'm sure we'll be back here again soon, but I feel sad about missing Christmas at Fortescue Manor.'

'Christmas here is always fun. But just think, you're going to Buckingham Palace! I can't wait to hear all about it. Oops, what's the time? I have to help at the laundry again.'

'Half-past five. I'll come with you.'

'Help at the laundry on your last evening in Shropshire? I'm sure you've got better things to do, Lottie!'

'No, I'd like to come.'

Chapter Fifty-One

Mrs Mallet was pleased to see them, and Rosie greeted her with a wagging tail. 'I think everyone wants everything freshly laundered in time for Christmas,' she said. 'I insist on paying you this time, Lottie.'

'No, there's no need. I'm here to keep Mildred company. We're not going to see each other for a while.'

'Lottie's going off to Buckingham Palace for Christmas,' Mildred said to her mother.

'Buckingham Palace?'

'It's just a Christmas ball. We're not staying there.'

'Just a Christmas ball? Well, I feel even more privileged to have you here with us, Lottie. From working in a laundry to Buckingham Palace within a few days! There can't be many people who can lay claim to that.'

Lottie and Mildred got to work taking dry laundry off the drying racks and folding it ready for ironing. Rosie made herself comfortable by the warm stove.

'I'm still not sure about Mrs Palmer,' said Lottie, as she

folded a shirt. 'She didn't like Ruth Campbell because she fired her from her job. And she also didn't like her sister-in-law, Lily Granger. And both of them are dead.'

'She can't have murdered Lily Granger,' said Mildred. 'She was locked up at the time.'

'Maybe her husband did?'

'Murdered his own sister?'

'Maybe. Perhaps Mrs Palmer murdered Ruth Campbell and her husband murdered Lily Granger.'

'And he found another gun?'

'He must have done.'

'So their reason for murdering Mrs Campbell and Mrs Granger is that they didn't like them?'

'Or bore them a grudge of some sort. We'll have to find out more about Lily Granger's relationship with her brother.'

'That won't be easy. And you're off to London tomorrow, Lottie.'

Lottie sighed. 'Don't remind me.'

'Look, here's a Father Christmas costume,' said Mildred as she folded a red jacket trimmed with fake white fur. 'Someone will be needing that again before Christmas.'

Mrs Mallet brought in some tea. 'You're making good progress,' she said. 'Now which one of you wants to do the ironing?'

'I'll give it a go,' said Mildred. 'But I'll be careful this time. I don't want to burn myself again.'

'No, you don't.'

'Another Father Christmas outfit,' said Lottie, as she folded a festive red jacket.

'Yes, it belongs to the mayor's office,' said Mrs Mallet. 'There are a lot of Christmas outfits at this time of year. I also launder costumes for the Christmas pantomime. It certainly beats all the boring plain linen that we do the rest of the year.'

'The mayor's office has two Father Christmas outfits?' said

Lottie, noticing that she'd placed it in the basket with the first one.

'I think so,' said Mrs Mallet. 'Are the laundry marks the same?'

Lottie checked the laundry labels. 'Yes.'

'He must have dressed up as Father Christmas for another event too,' said Mildred. 'Perhaps he's got a whole wardrobe of them for this time of year!'

Chapter Fifty-Two

'DETECTIVE INSPECTOR HANBURY from Scotland Yard will be here at ten o'clock,' said Lord Buckley-Phipps at breakfast the following morning. 'He wants everyone in the drawing room at that time and that includes all the members of the Lowton Chorley Ladies' Society.'

'All of them?' said Mrs Moore. 'He thinks it's one of them?'

'I don't know. I can only assume Detective Inspector Lloyd has furnished him with the facts of the case and he's already drawn some conclusions. I can't say I want any of those ladies under my roof. It sounds like they're all rather dangerous!'

'Are they going to be checked for weapons when they arrive?' said Barty.

'That's an excellent idea! We need to have Miss Hudson in the entrance hall checking their handbags.'

'Surely you're joking, Ivan!' said Mrs Moore.

'I'm not Roberta. Those ladies are lethal!'

'I'm sure they won't cause any trouble while they're here. I hope the detective doesn't go on for too long. Lottie and I need to leave for our train at eleven.'

'Duxbury will make sure your luggage is loaded into the car on time,' said Lord Buckley-Phipps.

'And I need to go to the bank,' said Lottie.

Lottie had lain awake during the night thinking about the case. She had a few questions on her mind and only an hour or two to get them answered.

'You need to go to the bank, Lottie? I'm not sure we have time.'

'Everything is packed.' She drained her cup of tea. 'I'll go now and make sure I'm back for ten o'clock.'

Chapter Fifty-Three

LOTTIE HAD UNDERESTIMATED HOW LONG it would take her and Rosie to get to the village and back in the snow. By the time she arrived in the drawing room at ten o'clock, she felt hot and flustered.

The room was already filled with people, most of them members of the Lowton Chorley Ladies' Society. The mayor was also present, as were the household servants. Detective Inspector Lloyd and Detective Inspector Hanbury from Scotland Yard stood by the Christmas tree. Everyone sat on chairs facing them.

Lottie recognised Detective Inspector Hanbury from his previous investigation at Fortescue Manor. She found Mrs Moore and sat next to her with Rosie.

'Well done for getting back in time, Lottie,' she said. 'If this drags on a bit, we'll have to make our excuses.'

Lord and Lady Buckley-Phipps entered the room and took their seats at the front. Then Detective Inspector Hanbury cleared his throat and addressed everyone. He was a thin man with a thick moustache and spectacles.

'I apologise for taking my time getting here. As you're

aware, I had to wait for the railway line to be cleared. In the meantime, though, my colleague Detective Inspector Lloyd has been doing an excellent job on this complex case.'

Lottie heard a few sniggers from people who didn't seem to agree.

'It's almost Christmas,' continued the detective. 'And it's a busy time for all of you. I'll do my best not to detain you, but I'm sure you appreciate I need to gather lots of facts within a short space of time. That's why I requested you all come here today. It will speed everything up. If all goes well this morning, I hope to be finished by lunchtime.'

'Lunchtime?' said a lady with bobbed grey hair. 'I can spare an hour and nothing more.'

'Same here!' piped up Mrs Moore.

'We've already had to traipse up the hill to get here,' said a lady with horn-rimmed spectacles. 'And when you consider we have to walk back down that way too, it's almost an hour just to get here and back.'

'I appreciate that it's inconvenient,' said Detective Inspector Hanbury. 'But it's important I have all the facts of the case.'

'Lloyd has had the facts of the case for a week now,' said the grey-haired lady. 'And what's he done with them? Nothing except arrest the wrong person.'

'You're lucky we turned up at all today, Detective,' said Annie Roberts.

The Lowton Chorley Ladies' Society was a tough audience. Lottie felt sure she could hurry things along with her own suggestion. Although she was nervous, she raised her hand.

'Excuse me,' she said. 'But I think I know who the murderer is.'

Detective Inspector Hanbury squinted at her through his spectacles. 'You again?'

'Yes, sir. Me again.'

He sighed. 'I don't really appreciate the interruption. However, I'm aware you were right last time, young miss. Perhaps you can tell me what you have on your mind? But please make it quick, we don't have a lot of time. Can you stand up please so we can all hear you properly.'

Lottie did so, feeling uncomfortable as everyone turned to look at her. 'I believe the murderer is Walter Campbell.'

Chapter Fifty-Four

'I BEG YOUR PARDON?' Walter Campbell sprung up out of his chair as if a flame had been placed beneath him. 'Do you realise the severity of your accusation, young lady?'

'I can only assume Miss Sprigg has an explanation,' said Detective Inspector Hanbury.

The mayor laughed. 'And I should like to hear it!'

'Are you sure about this, Lottie?' said Lord Buckley-Phipps. 'Why would the mayor kill his own wife?'

'Because he wanted to marry his mistress,' piped up the grey-haired lady.

'I don't think it was that simple,' said Lottie.

The mayor chuckled and folded his arms. 'Out with it then. But be aware, young lady, that you're wasting the time of a very distinguished detective of the Yard.'

'At the Christmas Fayre, I recall Lily Granger telling Mrs Moore and me about how the mayor and mayoress had recently improved their living situation,' Lottie said. 'She mentioned they'd moved into a large home, the former vicarage. And Mrs Campbell had a new motor car.'

'And your point is what?' said the mayor.

'I also heard the mayor's charity has struggled this year,' said Lottie. 'That's why the decision was made to donate all the proceeds from the Christmas Fayre to its funds. Mrs Granger told me her son's company had donated money to the charity, and the mayor's brother also said he'd made a large donation. So the question is, where did the money go?'

'Managing a charity can be complicated, Lottie,' said Lord Buckley-Phipps. 'Presumably the mayor funded causes differently this year.'

'But Lottie has a point,' said his wife. 'The hospital received significantly less from the mayor's charity this year.'

'Sometimes that happens, my lady,' said Walter Campbell. 'Donations ebb and flow and can't be relied upon as a regular source of income.'

'But when you consider the mayor has bought a large home and a fancy new car,' said Mrs Moore. 'It makes you wonder, doesn't it?'

'Wait a moment, what are you implying?' said Lord Buckley-Phipps. 'Are you suggesting the mayor misappropriated funds from his charity? I find that hard to believe.'

'It could be confirmed by examining the records,' said Lady Buckley-Phipps. 'Perhaps Lottie is onto something. But how does this relate to the murders of Mrs Campbell and Mrs Granger?'

'I think they both knew about his embezzlement,' said Lottie. 'And I think they were threatening to tell.'

'How did they know about it?' said Lady Buckley-Phipps.

'Mrs Granger mentioned her son worked at Russell Bank,' said Lottie. 'I saw Walter Campbell visiting the bank last week and that's why I visited the bank this morning. Young Philip Granger wasn't there because he's taking some time off due to his recent bereavement. But a colleague of his kindly telephoned him for me and he told me he'd noticed large sums of money being deposited into the mayor's bank account. It wasn't clear where the money had come from. He'd reported the concerns to his manager who seemed reluctant to do anything about it.'

'The manager of Russell Bank is my good friend Bobby Hamilton,' said the mayor.

'A friend of yours?' said Lord Buckley-Phipps. 'So that explains why he was happy to turn a blind eye.'

'Philip Granger didn't know what else to do, so he told his mother,' said Lottie. 'And I'm sure she told Ruth Campbell. Annie Roberts told me she'd witnessed at least one heated conversation between the two ladies. She said she heard money mentioned as well as Mrs Granger's son, Philip. Perhaps this was when Mrs Granger informed Mrs Campbell about the embezzlement of charity funds.'

The mayor laughed. 'This tale keeps getting better and better!'

'I think there could be truth in it,' said Annie Roberts. 'I witnessed two heated conversations between Ruth and Lily. Money was mentioned both times.'

The smile on the mayor's face faded a little.

'To begin with, Ruth Campbell probably didn't want anyone to know about the embezzlement,' said Lottie. 'She was benefiting from a nice new home and car. But then she found out about the affair between her husband and Miss Roberts. She might have enjoyed the lifestyle, but she was clearly hurt by his betrayal. She consulted a solicitor about a divorce. I suspect she was also planning to tell everyone about her husband's crime. It would have been the ultimate revenge.'

'This sounds plausible,' said Lord Buckley-Phipps. 'But there is a large flaw in your explanation, Lottie. Walter Campbell couldn't have possibly committed the crime. While his wife was murdered, he was in this very room, dressed as Father Christmas, handing out presents to all the village children.'

Chapter Fifty-Five

'THAT'S what I thought too, my lord,' said Lottie. 'Until I discovered two identical Father Christmas outfits in the village laundry. Mrs Mallet told me both outfits belonged to the mayor's office. This made me consider that two men could have worn the outfits at the same time. If those men were of similar build and concealed most of their faces with large bushy beards, then it could be difficult to tell them apart.'

'So the mayor asked someone else to pose as Father Christmas so he could carry out the crime?' said Lord Buckley-Phipps.

'Yes, I believe that's what happened.'

'And who was this other man?'

'I believe it was the mayor's brother, Frederick Campbell,' said Lottie. 'They have a similar height and build and I can imagine them being almost indistinguishable when both dressed as Father Christmas.'

The mayor laughed again. 'You have a wonderful imagination, Miss Sprigg!'

'I know Frederick Campbell was here at the house while the presents were being handed out because he told me and

Mrs Moore that he was going to come here to laugh at his brother in his Father Christmas outfit.'

'But wouldn't Frederick Campbell have come forward and expressed suspicions about the mayor's involvement in his wife's murder?' said Lord Buckley-Phipps.

'I don't believe the mayor told his brother what he was planning, my lord,' said Lottie. 'Presumably he asked him to take his place because he didn't want to do it and had other matters to see to instead. I doubt Frederick Campbell would have assumed the worst because it's hard to imagine a family member carrying out such a crime.'

'So two gentlemen were dressed as Father Christmas,' said Detective Inspector Hanbury. 'How did they ensure no one spotted there were two?'

'Jack the footman, who was Father Christmas's elf that afternoon, told me the mayor visited the bathroom on at least one occasion,' said Lottie. 'I think that's how they swapped the role.'

'So Walter went in and Frederick came out and no one noticed the difference?' said Mrs Moore.

'It seems so,' said Lottie. 'Although Jack told me that Father Christmas seemed quite grumpy and said very little. I suspect Frederick Campbell didn't say much because he was worried about giving himself away.'

'So are you suggesting, Lottie, that Walter Campbell dashed off down the secret tunnel to murder his wife while his brother gave out presents?'

'Yes, my lord.'

'But how did he know about the secret tunnel? No one in this household knew about it and we couldn't even find the key.'

'I can't be certain Walter Campbell knew about the secret tunnel, my lord,' said Lottie. 'However, around seventy-five years ago, his great-grandfather was valet to the then-Lord

Buckley-Phipps. Perhaps knowledge of the tunnel was not passed down through the Buckley-Phipps family, but maybe it was passed down the Campbell family. This could explain why the key was not in this house. It may have been in the possession of the Campbell family.'

'To get to the secret tunnel, the mayor had to get to the basement. Why didn't any of the servants see him wandering around down there?'

'Most of them were at the Fayre,' said Lottie. 'But Mrs Palmer was in the servants' hall and she was there when the mayor, dressed as Father Christmas, and Jack arrived with a sack of gifts for the servants. Then the mayor told Jack to go to the drawing room and make sure all the children were forming an orderly queue. He told Jack he'd join him once he'd visited the bathroom. Five minutes later, he arrived in the drawing room to hand out the presents to the children. I suspect it was Frederick Campbell who arrived in the drawing room. By that time, Walter Campbell was making his way through the tunnel to the grotto.'

'And how did he know his wife would be there?' asked Detective Inspector Hanbury.

'Ruth Campbell had received a note from a friend asking to meet at the grotto at half-past three. We don't know the name of the friend, but I suspect that note came from Walter Campbell.'

'But how could he be certain that there wouldn't be other witnesses in the grotto?' said Lady Buckley-Phipps. 'Other people had been visiting during the afternoon, and they might have been present when he intended to harm his wife.'

'I believe that's why he extinguished all the candles and lamps,' said Lottie. 'Anyone visiting would have been discouraged by the darkness and returned to the Fayre. However, Mrs Campbell believed she was meeting a friend there. So even though the grotto was in darkness, she would probably have lingered to wait for them.'

'So the mayor shot his own wife and then escaped back through the passageway?'

'I think so,' said Lottie. 'Then, when he was back in the laundry room, he hid the gun in the wash tub. After that, he went to the bathroom and waited for his brother there so they could swap roles again.'

'The gun!' said Lord Buckley-Phipps. 'How did he steal Mr Palmer's gun?'

'He didn't, my lord,' said Detective Inspector Lloyd. 'Please forgive me, I forgot to tell you about that. It turns out Mr Palmer's gun wasn't missing after all. He'd merely left it in his shed and forgotten he'd taken it there.'

'So no one took Mr Palmer's gun?'

'No. The mayor—sorry, the culprit must have used a gun from elsewhere. Perhaps it was even his own gun.'

Chapter Fifty-Six

'Well I never,' said Lord Buckley-Phipps. 'What do you make of all this, Campbell?'

The mayor stroked his moustache. 'Well, it's quite a tale. And if I had plotted such a plan, that would make me a very clever man indeed.'

'Yes, quite clever,' said Lord Buckley-Phipps. 'Are you as clever as that?'

'Of course I am, my lord.'

'So you *did* do it?'

'Took the money? I was intending to pay every penny of it back. It was a loan to myself. The Old Vicarage only comes up for sale once in a generation. I'd had my heart set on that property for a long time, and I didn't want to miss out. I loaned myself the money to buy it.'

'From the charity?'

'It was a loan! I was going to pay every penny back.'

'And the car?'

'Yes, and the car. I was planning to repay it all.'

'How?'

'By cashing in a few investments.'

'Couldn't the investments have been cashed in sooner? Then you wouldn't have needed to take money from the charity.'

'It was rather complicated. It would have taken some time. You know how banks can be with their administrative processes... very slow indeed. So it made sense to access the money from the charity funds and then repay it. I realise now it wasn't a sensible or honourable decision. I must admit, I'm not the perfect mayor. But I did what I thought was best at the time.'

'No, you didn't!' said Lady Buckley-Phipps. 'You stole the charity's money! Just think of all those needy people and children who could have benefited from it! That money was intended for the people of this village. But you selfishly used it for yourself. You shouldn't have been buying the Old Vicarage. You were living beyond your means.'

'I have the money in investments, my lady,' said the mayor.

'Where? We need to see evidence of this. And even if you are able to repay that money, it can't change what you did. You stole from a charity which you were entrusted with. You helped yourself to the money to fund your own lifestyle. I don't believe you can repay it through investments. The only way to repay it is by selling your house and car!'

'Now, hold on, my lady, I'm sure we can come to some arrangement.'

Detective Inspector Hanbury intervened. 'I think this is a discussion for later. Mr Campbell, you admit you stole the money, but what about the murder of your wife, Ruth Campbell, and Lily Granger? Is Miss Sprigg correct? Did they confront you about the money?'

The mayor slumped down into his chair. 'Yes, Ruth challenged me about it.'

'What was she going to do?' inquired Lord Buckley-Phipps.

'She told me she was going to make an example of me. She threatened to ruin me. She claimed to have discovered other things about me too, and I can only guess now that she meant the affair. She didn't mention divorce at the time, but I think it's clear now why she wanted to divorce me.'

'So you murdered your wife to prevent her from revealing the embezzlement?'

'I didn't want to be ruined, and that's what she was threatening me with. She also told me that Lily Granger had told her about the embezzlement. Her son had spotted something wrong with the accounts. I didn't worry too much about her son, he was just a junior bank clerk and I knew Bobby could keep him quiet if required. But after Lily told Ruth, I realised they could tell more people. So, I suppose I do admit to silencing them. On reflection, I suppose matters got a little out of hand.'

'More than a little out of hand!' said Lord Buckley-Phipps. 'You're a thief and a murderer and I'm ashamed to have ever known you!'

'Did you know about the secret tunnel, Mr Campbell?' asked Detective Inspector Hanbury.

'Yes. My father told me about it and I inherited the key from him. It was a Campbell family secret. And I kept it quiet because I had a feeling I could use it to my advantage one day.'

'Did your brother know about it?'

'I don't think he did. Being the older of the two and inheriting my father's belongings, I was told the secret and given the key. I once secretly visited the grotto and found the door to the tunnel at the back. I walked along the tunnel, found the door at the end, and was delighted to find my key worked in the lock. From that moment, I thought about a day when I could use the tunnel to set a trap for someone I didn't like. Ruth wasn't the first person I'd considered it for. There have been others in the past who frustrated me to the point where I thought it would be a good place to commit a crime. But Ruth became a threat to me and the problem had to be dealt with.'

'What did you tell your brother Frederick to persuade him to be Father Christmas?' asked Lord Buckley-Phipps.

'I simply asked him for a favour for an hour. I told him I didn't like children, which is actually true. It was a believable excuse. I explained it was my first Christmas Fayre as mayor, and I had to spend my time with the important people, not waste it with the village children. He has his own children and grandchildren and was happy to help. I know he'll be extremely disappointed when he learns what I've done. Miss Sprigg is right, Frederick would never have imagined I was capable of such a thing. I can assure you he knew nothing about my actual plan. All he knew was that he switched into my role for a bit, and nobody noticed. But he had no idea what I was planning.

'My tenure as mayor was going well, and I didn't want to lose my position. Ruth and I fell out shortly after we got married and, despite my pretence, you all now realise it wasn't a happy marriage. I acknowledge my actions were extreme, but I acted out of self-preservation. I sent Ruth a note asking to meet at the grotto. I pretended Lily Granger had sent the note. How happy I was Lily discovered her! I believed everyone would assume she was the culprit because of their rivalry.'

'And you felt the need to silence Mrs Granger as well?'

'Yes, I knew what she was like. It wouldn't be long before she told people about my financial affairs. I couldn't risk word getting out. I suppose I'm guilty of trying to protect my repu-tation a little too much.'

'And the gun?'

'I've got lots of guns, Detective. I like to use them for

target practice. It's a shame I lost one by having to leave it in the wash tub. I wiped my fingerprints off it, as you probably discovered. I thought it was a clever plan. Too clever for anyone else to work out. But, unfortunately for me, I was mistaken.'

Chapter Fifty-Seven

WALTER CAMPBELL WAS LED AWAY in handcuffs and the Lowton Chorley Ladies' Society made their way back down the hill to the village.

The Buckley-Phipps family retired to the sitting room.

'My dear old friend Walter Campbell.' Lord Buckley-Phipps shook his head. 'I never would have imagined it. What a thing to do! And to put all that planning into it as well. It's cruel and barbaric.'

'But he always was a bit of a funny one, Ivan,' said Lady Buckley-Phipps.

'Well, if you thought that, Lucinda, perhaps you could have warned me off him! I always thought you liked him.'

'I quite liked him. But there was always something odd about him. Having said that, I never would have imagined he would murder two people.'

'Dreadful. The man clearly thought he could do whatever he wanted. As soon as he was elected mayor, all the power went to his head. The next mayor will have to be carefully vetted indeed.'

'Well, at least we can sell his house now and donate all the funds to charity. And then they can be distributed throughout the area for the benefit of all.'

'Yes, that's something good that can come out of this, Lucinda,' said Mrs Moore. 'The people who deserve that money will receive it.'

'Oh, good heavens!' said Lady Buckley-Phipps. 'I've just realised the time. You need to be taken to the station, Roberta.'

Lottie glanced at the clock on the mantelpiece. It was quarter past eleven.

'Too late,' said Mrs Moore. 'We've missed our train.'

'But there must be a later one you can get!'

'Yes, I suppose there will be. But you know me, Lucinda, I don't like rushing about.'

'But the ball is tomorrow! How will you get there in time?'

'I don't think we will. And besides, people are saying more snow is on the way. I don't like the idea of being stranded en route to London.'

'But you've been invited to Buckingham Palace! It's a once-in-a-lifetime opportunity!'

'You're right, Lucinda, it is. But I'll only know a few people there. And all this business over the past week has tired me out. It's left me feeling a little too weary for all that social-ising in London. I know that as soon as I'm there, I'll feel obliged to call on friends and go to parties and generally spread myself about like butter on a piece of bread. I really don't think I've got the energy.'

'So you're passing up the opportunity to attend the Christmas ball at the palace?'

'Yes, I'm afraid I am.' Mrs Moore turned to Lottie. 'I'm sorry, Lottie. I know how much you were looking forward to it.'

Lottie didn't mind at all. In fact, she felt quite pleased that they wouldn't be travelling to London. 'Please don't worry, Mrs Moore. I'm sure there will be other invitations.'

'Yes, I'm sure there will be. I shall telephone my apologies to my dear friend. Hopefully, my name will remain on a list for a palace party in the future.'

Chapter Fifty-Eight

'Ready, steady, go!'

Rosie gave an excited bark, and the two toboggans set off down the snowy hill. Lottie clung on with one hand and held Rosie with the other. Mildred sat in front of her, whooping as the sledge picked up speed.

Lottie glanced across at their competitors. Edward the footman was steering the sledge while Jack sat behind him, urging him to go faster.

The cold air chilled Lottie's face as they hurtled down the slope towards Fortescue Manor. Warm lights glimmered in its windows.

Jack and Edward edged ahead of them.

'We'll catch you!' called out Mildred. 'Just you see!'

The sledge bounced and lurched as they picked up speed. Lottie wasn't too alarmed. There was no gingerbread stall to crash into this time. But she caught sight of two figures walking across the bottom of the slope towards the lake.

There was a shout and Lottie saw Jack and Edward's sledge tip over. They tumbled into the snow, laughing.

'Bye!' said Mildred as they raced on past. Lottie glanced

back to see the two young men climbing back onto their sledge. They'd catch up with them soon enough.

Rosie's tongue lolled out of her mouth and Lottie laughed at how unbothered she was by the speed they were travelling at.

The two figures were closer now.

'They need to move!' shouted Mildred.

One was a tall lanky gentleman in an overcoat, hat and scarf. 'Is that Barty?' cried out Lottie.

'Yes! Who's he with?'

'I think that's Evelyn Abercromby!'

The couple had noticed the toboggan hurtling towards them and were now doing their best to skip out of the way.

'Watch out!' came a shout from behind.

Lottie turned to see Jack and Edward directly behind them.

Barty and Evelyn moved faster as both sledges hurtled directly at them.

'Oh no!' said Lottie. 'They're not moving fast enough! Can't you steer around them?'

'Steer? How do I steer?'

'I don't know!'

Barty and Evelyn jumped to the left as Lottie and Mildred leaned to the right. Fortunately, the sledge avoided them, but Lottie and Mildred had leaned too far. The sledge tipped over and they fell into the snow. Rosie jumped clear and Lottie rolled over in the snow.

She glimpsed Jack deliberately tumbling off his sledge. Edward continued on down the slope.

'Are you alright?' asked Jack.

'I'm fine!'

Then something hit the back of Lottie's woolly hat.

A snowball.

She turned to see Barty laughing at her. She gathered up a

ball of snow in her gloved hands, then hurled it at him. It hit Barty in the chest, and Evelyn laughed.

Mildred and Jack joined in with the snowball fight and Rosie ran around in circles, barking with excitement.

'Oi!' The shout came from the bottom of the slope. 'What about me?' Edward was feeling left out.

'Come and join us!' said Barty. 'We're going to bury Jack in the snow!'

'Just you try!' said Jack. He hurled a snowball at Barty, but Rosie jumped up and caught it in her mouth.

'Saved by a corgi!' said Barty.

'I need to warm up,' said Mildred. 'Mrs Palmer said she would make a big pan of hot chocolate. Shall we go and see if it's ready yet?'

'Yes!' said Lottie.

Everyone began to make their way towards the warm lights of Fortescue Manor.

THE END

* * *

Thank you

Thank you for reading this Lottie Sprigg mystery. I really hope you enjoyed it! Here are a few ways to stay in touch:

- Join my mailing list and receive a FREE short story *Murder at the Castle*: marthabond.com/murder-at-the-castle
- Like my brand new Facebook page: facebook.com/marthabondauthor

A free Lottie Sprigg mystery

Find out what happens when Lottie, Rosie and Mrs Moore visit Scotland in this free mystery _Murder at the Castle_!

When Lottie Sprigg accompanies her employer to New Year celebrations in a Scottish castle, she's excited about her first ever Hogmanay. The guests are in party spirits and enjoying the pipe band, dancing and whisky.

But the mood turns when a guest is found dead in the billiard room. Who committed the crime? With the local police stuck in the snow, Lottie puts her sleuthing skills to the test. She makes good progress until someone takes drastic action to stop her uncovering the truth...

Visit my website to claim your free copy:

marthabond.com/murder-at-the-castle

Or scan the code on the following page:

Murder in the Maze

Book 3 in the Lottie Sprigg Country House Mystery Series!

A West End starlet and her aristocrat husband are hosting a birthday party at their Buckinghamshire home. With a guest list from *Who's Who*, it's the most fashionable event of the season. Young sleuth, Lottie Sprigg, is excited to accompany her employer there; even if she feels a little out of place.

All visitors to the house are keen to explore the tricky maze. How long will it take to find their way out? It's a challenge everyone takes on. Until one unlucky guest never finds their way out at all...

A murderer has struck in the maze! With the help of her four-legged friend Rosie, Lottie investigates. But as the case twists and turns, it's not long until she finds herself at a dead end. How can she find her way out of the puzzle? With the killer still at large, it proves to be a dangerous undertaking.

Get your copy: mybook.to/murder-maze

Also by Martha Bond

Lottie Sprigg Country House Mystery Series:

Murder in the Library
Murder in the Grotto
Murder in the Maze

Lottie Sprigg Travels Mystery Series:

Murder in Venice
Murder in Paris
Murder in Cairo
Murder in Monaco
Murder in Vienna

Writing as Emily Organ:

Augusta Peel Mystery Series:

Death in Soho
Murder in the Air

The Bloomsbury Murder
The Tower Bridge Murder
Death in Westminster

Penny Green Mystery Series:

Limelight
The Rookery
The Maid's Secret
The Inventor
Curse of the Poppy
The Bermondsey Poisoner
An Unwelcome Guest
Death at the Workhouse
The Gang of St Bride's
Murder in Ratcliffe
The Egyptian Mystery
The Camden Spiritualist

Churchill & Pemberley Mystery Series:

Tragedy at Piddleton Hotel
Murder in Cold Mud
Puzzle in Poppleford Wood
Trouble in the Churchyard
Wheels of Peril
The Poisoned Peer
Fiasco at the Jam Factory
Disaster at the Christmas Dinner
Christmas Calamity at the Vicarage (novella)

Made in United States
Orlando, FL
03 April 2024

45430222R00129